Heart's Perilous Journey

WAGON TRAIN MATCHES
BOOK EIGHT

LACY WILLIAMS

One

"IT'S BEEN TWO DAYS."

Alice glanced up from the cast iron skillet on the camp fire, where she was frying up some venison, to where her brothers Leo, Collin, and Owen stood close to one of the Conestoga wagons that had carried them West from Independence, Missouri.

Morning light was breaking over the circled wagons. Over seventy conveyances and more than twice that many travelers. Men, women and children, some still sleeping in tents or bedrolls beneath their wagons, some stirring to tend fires or check on oxen and horses. Nearby, a chicken clucked and a snuffle of a dog's bark responded.

Months had passed on the trail. Difficult weeks filled with danger—hunting their own food, bad weather, herding cattle meant for their future, and men hunting the pioneers. The same sheer exhaustion Alice felt showed in the men's faces. Leo had grown tan under the constant sunshine. Collin couldn't stop sending glances to where his wife rested in a nearby wagon, fighting for her life after being shot during a recent skirmish. A frown was etched into Owen's expression.

August was setting up camp with his wife Felicity and the little girl they'd adopted, Ben.

And there was one other brother missing. Coop.

His absence vibrated like a constant hum beneath Alice's skin. The last time she'd seen him, there'd been chaos. Gunshots ringing out as hired mercenaries had attacked their wagon train. Screams from terrified men and women. Two wagons had careened past the others, the oxen pulling them out of control and racing away—and Coop had ridden after them on horseback. Been separated from the company.

That had to be why her brothers were huddled together, why they were so serious.

Rob—Mr. Braddock is out there, too, her mind whispered.

As the two wagons had raced away from the company, an explosion and rockslide had separated them. One of those wagons belonged to the man Alice and her brothers had worked for back in New Jersey, Robert Braddock.

The same man who would've seen Coop thrown in prison for a terrible accident that had happened in the Braddock gunpowder mills.

The same man who'd once told her he'd needed her, whom she'd imagined herself falling in love with.

Coop and Rob had been in several scuffles since the company had departed from Independence. One of those fights had been a walloping—Rob had limped around with bruises on his face for days after.

And Alice couldn't help wondering whether the two men

had run into trouble out in the woods—and whether that trouble was each other. Coop wore a pistol. Rob kept a rifle. What if they'd gotten into another fight?

She couldn't bear to think it.

She left the meat in the frying pan over the hot coals and approached her brothers' huddle so she could hear what they were discussing.

"Coop might be hurt. Maddie 'n Jason's wagon crashed so bad its axle broke."

"He was on horseback," Leo said grimly. "He should've stayed on the trail and ridden to get help."

Leo's voice held both expectation and frustration. Coop had a difficult time with his oldest brother's leadership. He often bucked Leo's orders.

"There had to have been a reason he and Braddock took off into the woods," Collin argued. He and Coop were twins and had been thick as thieves since birth. Sometimes it seemed like they knew what each other was thinking—a trick they'd used on Alice more than once during their teenage years. But lately, there'd been a distance between them. Ever since Collin had married Stella a few weeks into their journey.

Collin's eyes strayed to the wagon where his injured wife rested. Stella had taken a bullet to the abdomen during the recent attack. She'd survived a terrible surgery but still fought off infection. Collin must be plenty worried about Coop to have left her side—he hadn't gone more than a few feet from her since the company had ridden out of that valley.

"Plenty of wildlife the two men could've run into out there." This from Owen. The half-brother she hadn't known existed until five months ago.

Alice and Leo's father had divorced their mother and abandoned their family when Alice had been a newborn babe. He'd gone to find his fortune in California. There he'd fathered two boys. Owen and August.

Leo and Alice hadn't known their father's whereabouts, or even if he was still alive. After his death, Owen and August had come East to find their half siblings and make things right that their father never had.

It was Owen's idea that the Spencer siblings disappear into the wilds of Oregon so that Coop might avoid prison.

A few paces away, August stood with his back to the group, one hand gripping the handle of the coffeepot that hung over the fire. His other hand hovered in the air, fingers spread as if trying to sense the location of his tin cup on the ground beside him.

Alice's feet moved before her mind caught up. She'd barely taken two steps when August's jaw tightened.

"I can manage," he said, his voice low but firm.

She froze mid-stride. "I was only—"

"I don't need your help, Alice." The words came out clipped, almost harsh. August finally located his cup, his movements careful and deliberate as he lifted the pot.

The coffee sloshed as he poured, some of it missing the cup entirely and hissing against the hot stones circling the fire. August's mouth pressed into a thin line, but he said nothing. Just set the pot down with more force than necessary and turned away, the cup cradled in both hands.

Alice stood rooted to the spot, her throat tight. She'd only wanted to—

What? Fix things? Make it easier? As if her help could restore what he'd lost.

An ache settled in her chest as she returned to her brothers' huddle.

"Maybe he doesn't want to be found." Leo's voice was tight and angry.

Alice tucked her hands into her apron pockets, fingers curling into loose fists.

Leo had stopped confiding in her months ago—even before they'd left New Jersey. She knew about the promise he'd made Ma on her deathbed. A promise to keep the family together, to protect his younger brothers.

Leo didn't know that Alice had made a vow of her own back in New Jersey. To bring Coop back into the fold. Her brother had fallen in with some bad friends. Broken promises, gambled, boxed for money. But Coop wasn't a bad person. Leo may have given up on him, but Alice never would. She opened her mouth to say as much but was interrupted.

"What do you want to do?" Owen asked Leo. "Hollis says we can't delay another day. Snow's coming and we can't afford to get trapped in the mountains."

She'd felt the chill this morning, while dressing in her tent in the dark. Still had her shawl wrapped around her shoulders. A nip of winter was in the air.

And Coop and Rob remained somewhere out there, without supplies or the protection of the wagon train.

"I'll go after him." Even she could hear the reluctance in Collin's voice. He loved Stella deeply, didn't want to be away from her.

Leo's hands clenched into fists at his sides. "Maybe it's time we stopped cleaning up his messes. Let him find his way back to the company."

Her heart pounded in her chest at her brother's callous words. She moved toward the group. "Leo—"

He looked surprised to find her close enough to hear. Owen's eyes shadowed when he looked at Alice.

"We can't leave the two of them out there alone," she said as she joined their circle. She was careful not to say Mr. Braddock's name. None of her brothers knew what had transpired between her and the wealthy mill owner back in New Jersey. Leo and Collin both hated the man for his part in ostracizing and prosecuting Coop.

"Hollis is right about the snows," Owen said gently.

"And so what happens to two men out here if the snows come?" she demanded.

"They probably just need a day or two to catch up to the company," Leo said. Though even he didn't sound too certain.

"Then why haven't they already made it?"

Leo reached out to pat her shoulder. "It ain't worth getting so upset."

Something was wrong. She could feel it.

"Leo, I think—"

He gave her shoulder a tiny brotherly shake. "Let us figure this out. Lotsa folks need reassurance this morning. Why don't you check on Ben and Felicity?"

He wasn't listening to her. Was ready to dismiss her.

She was opening her mouth to argue when she caught Owen's slight headshake. Was no one here going to be level-headed? They couldn't leave behind their *brother*.

But it couldn't be more obvious that her presence in this discussion was unwanted.

Chest cinched tight, she turned on her heel and marched off.

But she didn't go back to the fire. At this moment, she didn't care if their breakfast burned to ash.

She rounded the wagon so she was out of sight of her brothers and slipped around to where Stella rested. There was a soft murmur of voices—was Stella awake?

Alice went on tiptoe to peer into the open canvas at the back of the wagon. It was a tight squeeze inside. Although some of Stella and Collin and Stella's sister Lily's belongings had been moved to Leo's wagon, stacked crates and boxes carefully surrounded the pallet inside. Jason Goodwin, the camp doctor and Stella's brother-in-law, perched with one knee on the tailgate, checking on his patient.

Alice shored up her smile at the sight of the plucky, independent young woman pale against the pillow.

"How are you feeling this morning?" Alice asked gently.

"Right as rain," came Stella's faint answer. She had a faint flush on her cheeks. "I'll be up from this bed before you know it."

Jason's gaze was hooded. After Collin and Stella had married, the Spencers and the Fairfax sisters had become close. Everyone knew that the threat of infection and fever might still overcome Stella, strong as she was. And she was carrying a baby.

Alice held her breath but then let it out in a rush. "Can I borrow your horse?"

Maddie rounded the wagon, glancing curiously at Alice. She must've heard.

Stella's brows drew together. "Duncan? What for?"

"I'm going after Coop."

Now it was Jason's brow that furrowed. "Who's going with you?"

Alice kicked her chin up a notch. "I rode to the fort alone when everyone else was sick." It was a white lie. She'd ridden with Rob, though he'd been so pale and sick she hadn't been entirely sure he would make it.

"You aren't going." When had Collin snuck up behind her?

Maddie and Jason exchanged a loaded look.

"There's—someone else was inside my wagon before it got separated from the company," Maddie said slowly. "A young woman named Belle."

"A runaway," Jason added.

"Even more reason for a woman to go fetch them back," Alice said.

Collin crossed his arms over his chest. "You aren't going, and that's final."

Alice had failed at keeping her family together so far. She couldn't fail at this. Coop couldn't be left behind. But she tried not to think what it would mean to be in close quarters with Rob once the men were found.

She aimed her best big-sister glare at her brother. "You can't stop me."

* * *

Rob Braddock roused in a haze of intense pain. He felt it everywhere, but it seemed to start at his leg and radiate outward.

He opened his eyes as awareness intruded on the darkness. He was lashed to a dark brown horse, upright, with ropes securing both legs to the saddle. Cold seeped through his clothes. They had no blankets, no way to build a fire even if they dared stop.

Something hot trickled from the wound in his leg. Or was that an imagining? He tipped his head but only saw the fabric Coop Spencer had used to wrap the wound.

Coop.

Anger hotter than his wound flared. Coop had gotten Rob into this mess.

Though it wasn't Coop's fault that Rob was injured—not directly.

The horse climbed a shallow incline and the movement jostled Rob's leg. White-hot pain flared through him. He gritted his teeth against the scream that wanted to escape.

Alice. Think of Alice.

The woman he loved was with the wagon train. He could only pray she was safe.

Rob suppressed a groan as his gaze glanced off of the young woman on Coop's horse. It was difficult to hold his focus, but he thought she looked the same as she had the past three days that they'd been separated from the company. Pale and frightened. Jumpy. Startling at every leaf that dropped. He'd never seen her as part of the wagon train, but Coop knew her somehow. She must be the young woman who'd been skulking around camp, who'd run into the woods when Rob had come upon Coop once at last light.

Someone—a man—had been after her. The man who hunted Coop and Rob, had shot at them, tried to kill them. He'd nearly succeeded. When Rob had gone off that cliff's edge, he'd thought he was done for.

Until he'd woken lying in an icy stream, leg and ribs screaming in pain.

Jason Goodwin, the doctor back at camp, could put Rob back together. Back at camp, there would also be warm food, clean bandages, shelter. Out here, they had nothing but the horses and whatever ammunition remained in Coop's gun.

His pain spiked again, and within, that feeling of something hot running down his leg. He must've gasped, or else Coop just sensed his distress, because the other man turned his head from where he led Rob's horse.

"I gotta get down," Rob's shaky words were barely above a whisper.

The girl, Belle, jumped anyway. Her gaze flew to him and then scanned their surroundings, like she was expecting the man with the gun to jump out of the woods.

Coop slowed his steps so that he came alongside the horse's shoulder. "We can't afford to stop."

Rob felt as if the top of his head was floating away. From the blood he'd lost? From hunger? None of them had eaten since yesterday morning. "I gotta lie down."

Coop frowned. He looked exhausted, lines deepened around his mouth and eyes. His face was gaunt, hollowed by days without proper food or rest. A patch of dried blood colored his upper left sleeve, where he'd been winged by that shooter's bullet. He glanced at the girl, whose eyes skittered away nervously.

"The shooter could still be out there," he mumbled.

"No way he survived the fall and that rushing stream," Rob argued, voice raspy.

"We don't know that."

Why couldn't Coop just listen to reason? "I barely survived," Rob growled. For a moment, he felt the grip of the icy water as he came to, the jolt of pain and adrenaline and fear.

"We didn't find his body," Coop said.

"He'll never give up." Belle's voice, clear as a chime, drew both men's gazes. "Not while I'm alive."

Rob was a little unclear on why the man was after her. She'd barely said a word since Coop had pulled her out of the wagon with the busted axle. Rob had never seen anyone so scared before.

And it was obvious Coop believed her.

The pain in Rob's leg intensified, radiating outward, crawling up his spine, bursting bright lights behind his eyes. He flared hot and then cold. Heard Coop muttering from a far distance. Had a sense that the horse was being drawn to a stop, that there was motion around his legs. What was Coop doing? Untying him?

Rob hated having to rely on Coop. Coop was the one who'd been drinking on the job back at the Braddock Powder Mills in New Jersey. He'd been the cause of an explosion that had cost two lives and knocked down an entire building. The man was a menace.

Instead of allowing him to face the consequences of his

actions, Coop's family had run. They'd up and left to go West, joined Hollis's wagon train in Independence.

It'd taken two private investigators to find out where Alice had disappeared to. Rob had rushed his own preparations, had nearly missed his chance to join the wagon train.

Too weak to do anything else, he slumped against Coop as the other man helped him from the saddle. Rob didn't make it two steps from the horse before his good leg collapsed under him. Even with Coop taking most of his weight, there was not enough strength left in Rob's limbs to do anything other than fold to the ground.

Fire raced up his leg and spine as Coop straightened his broken leg in front of him. Coop had tried to splint it, but the ties must've come loose.

Perhaps he blacked out, because when he came to, the edges of his vision were shadowy and the girl was leaning over him. Her mouth was moving, but he couldn't hear what she said over the roar of pain in his head.

Something wet dribbled against his chin. Water, he realized through the murky haze. He managed to open his mouth, swallowed some of it. When it hit his stomach, he felt the cavernous emptiness inside. When was the last time he'd eaten? Before they'd been separated from the company, from all his supplies...

"—burning up—" A snatch of Coop's voice broke through, and Rob realized he'd drifted off again.

Was there a wildfire nearby? Like the one they'd barely survived on the plains?

Blackness grabbed hold of him again, a reprieve from the constant, throbbing pain.

He woke with a sense of wrongness cutting through the pain in his leg. What had alerted him?

It took far too long for him to pry open his eyes. Too long to register that the sky had grown darker. Was it evening? Or morning? Had he blacked out for that long?

Coop was nowhere in sight, but Belle sat a few feet away, her back to a thick tree, knees drawn up to her chest and her tattered shawl wrapped around all of her. Her eyes were glued to the growing shadows across the small clearing.

Where was Coop?

He tried to make his mouth work, tried to move, but his limbs felt sluggish and heavy. Everything hurt, his leg worst of all.

A branch snapped from several yards away.

Belle wasn't frozen. He could see her entire body trembling as she stared in the direction that noise had come from.

It took everything Rob had for him to wiggle his right pinky. He patted the ground near his hip. Coop must've taken off Rob's gun belt when he'd laid him out on the ground here, but his finger connected with the cold metal of his revolver. With a herculean effort, he slipped it out of the holster and pushed up on his left elbow.

"I'm guessing Coop didn't head out in that direction?" Garbled, mumbled words, but somehow Belle understood him because she shook her head. He glimpsed a flash of silver off the knife she held in her fisted hand, just visible under the fringe of the shawl.

He raised the gun in his weak, shaking hand. Pointed it at the woods.

Maybe he couldn't walk. Maybe he was a sitting duck,

waiting to be shot. But he wasn't about to let that shooter take Belle without a fight.

His finger tightened on the trigger as a man's body separated from the shadows between two trees.

His eyes were playing tricks on him. Had to be.

Because that man looked like Leo Spencer.

Two

ALICE'S HORSE was only a few paces behind Leo when he slipped from the saddle and pulled his rifle from its scabbard.

She peered through the gloom and caught movement in a little clearing ahead.

Leo gestured her to stay back as Doc came alongside her.

Was that...?

Leo called out at the same moment she recognized Rob lying on the ground, holding a gun on her brother.

She opened her mouth to cry out or to scream—she didn't know which—but Rob dropped his gun arm and then slumped to the ground.

Alice didn't register how she got down from her borrowed horse, but she closed the distance between her and Leo and followed him into the clearing.

Almost as soon as they passed the treeline, Coop emerged from the woods to their right. A young woman—Belle?—

huddled a few feet from Rob. Alice had thought her a part of the shadowy landscape until this moment.

"What happened?" Leo's demand seemed to encompass all three people.

From the corner of her eye, she caught the way Coop went tense, even as he holstered a revolver at his hip.

"Took a little spill," Rob called out.

He was alive. But why didn't he get up? Doc moved in his direction while Alice went to Coop and threw her arms around his shoulders.

He flinched, and as he moved back, she saw the rust-colored stain on his left upper arm.

"What happened?" she asked. "Were you shot?"

Coop's gaze flicked to Leo, who must've walked up behind Alice, and then back to her. "We ran into some trouble. Thought to cut through the woods and meet up with Hollis and the others—"

A muffled, sharp word from Rob. She hadn't meant to look at him at all, but her body didn't get the message because she turned and now couldn't help but notice the blood soaked bandages around his upper leg.

Doc's gaze alternated between her and Leo. "Leg's busted pretty bad. Alice, I'm going to need help. Leo, a fire."

Her older brother took a moment to make sure the horses were secured and then took a hatchet from a loop on his saddle and moved off to the clearing's edge, presumably to get some kindling. He pointed the end of the hatchet at Coop as he walked. "You're not finished telling me what happened."

She took a steadying breath and joined Doc on the oppo-site side of Rob's leg. A distinct scent—not a pleasant one—

came from the wound. Her gaze flew to Doc's face, only to find his expression guarded and serious.

"Where's my hug?" Rob rasped. His eyes were closed, head tipped back. How had he known she'd come near? Lines of pain bracketed his mouth.

She ignored his query. Let her gaze flick to the young woman who huddled in such a tight ball that it looked like she wanted to disappear into herself. She held something clutched in one hand—was that a knife?

"Is she all right?" she barely breathed the question to Doc, who gave the slightest shrug. He had wholly focused on Rob.

She could hear snatches of Coop's terse explanation to Leo. Something about having a feeling someone was following them, a shootout, and Rob getting pushed off a cliffside—?

"You fell off a cliff?" she asked. It was a wonder he'd survived at all.

"Mostly hit the water—a creek running through." Rob's eyes remained closed.

"He's got a high fever." Doc cut away the fabric of Rob's pant leg below his knee.

"Figured it was the better choice," Rob mumbled as if the doc hadn't spoken. "'Stead of letting your brother get shot."

Her breath caught, stomach knotting at the thought. She didn't dare examine too closely whether the thought of Coop or Rob injured was causing her distress.

"You've got some infection in the wound," Doc told Rob. "That's what's causing your fever." To Alice. "I'll need to clean it out as best I can before I stitch him up."

Leo came near and dropped a large armful of wood on the ground with a clatter.

The young woman jumped, but Rob didn't even seem to register the startling noise.

"I'm going to need clean water," Doc said. "As much of it as I can get. And that fire started now. Alice, can you check my saddlebag? Bring any clean cloth you can find."

At the horses, she took a second to gather herself. It was a bad sign that Rob wasn't moving. Maybe she'd believed she was falling for him, once upon a time, but those feelings were long over. She might not feel anything for the man—but that didn't mean she wanted him dead.

Alice fumbled through Doc's saddlebag until her fingers found strips of clean linen. Behind her, Leo's voice rose sharp, then Coop's lower rumble cut across it. She couldn't make out the words, but the tension carried clear enough.

When she turned back, Coop was gesturing—not at Rob, but at Belle. Alice caught the tail end of his glance in the girl's direction before Leo stepped into his line of sight, blocking whatever silent exchange had passed between them.

"Belle." Doc's tone was gentle as Alice knelt beside him. "I need you to fetch some water. We splashed through a creek a few yards back."

The girl's head shook. Her knees drew up tighter to her chest, face disappearing against them.

Doc's jaw worked. When he looked at Alice, something grim flickered across his face.

The girl couldn't help. Or wouldn't, maybe.

"I'll get it," Alice said quietly.

"Hurry." Doc was already reaching for the sodden bandages around Rob's thigh.

When she rushed back to the clearing with the water, a

small fire was burning and Leo was nowhere in sight. Coop was prowling the edges of the clearing, peering into the darkness.

When she rushed to put the water pail into the edge of the fire to heat it, the scent from Rob's leg hit.

His face had gone pale and he was breathing shallow and fast.

"Infection's set in deep." Doc probed the edges of the wound. "I've got to clean this out before I can stitch you up."

"Do it," Rob said through gritted teeth.

As Doc poured disinfectant over the wound, Rob's body went rigid and then slack. His head lolled to the side.

"Rob?" Alice hadn't meant for her voice to quaver.

"He's out." Doc didn't look up, hands still moving with steady efficiency. "Better for him. Alice, I need more water. And those cloths."

She handed Doc the clean linen before getting up to fetch another pail of water. Striding into the growing darkness, she couldn't help but shiver. Was the person who'd attacked Rob and Coop still out there somewhere?

They wouldn't be safe until they returned to the company. But how could Rob be moved with his leg in such bad shape?

* * *

Everything was shadows and darkness. Light flickered from a lantern hung on the wall outside the two-story building, but it didn't reach the place where she was hunkered down, hidden inside the horse's stall in this lean-to. The lean-to had been a late addition to the barn and a hasty one at that. There were big cracks between the planks in the wall, knotholes big enough for her to peer out of. Only inches behind her, the horse blew softly. It was dangerous to crouch here, between the animal's hooves and the wall.

But even more dangerous to be outside. With him there.

Grateful she'd seen him before he'd known she was outside, she shivered in the chill evening, wrapped her threadbare shawl around her. She'd be missed before long. A trip to the privy wasn't meant to take more than a couple of minutes.

Thaddeus, the owner of this so-called establishment might come out that door any moment, calling out for her. Or maybe he'd send Virgil, his son. The boy was all of nineteen, a whole year older than her, all muscle and no brain. At least that's what Pretty said.

Belle had learned not to say anything.

"I'm Alice Spencer. Coop's sister."

The quiet introduction startled Belle out of her memories. It took her a moment in the flickering firelight to remember her surroundings.

Not trapped at the brothel. Not any longer. She was in the woods, some miles from where she'd snuck into a wagon piled with goods and left behind the life she'd known since she was fourteen years old.

She'd spent so much time hiding in empty wagons when folks weren't paying attention, sneaking through the woods to keep watch, scrounging for any bite of food she might nick... Time ebbed and flowed. Had it been weeks since she'd stowed away with this wagon train? Or merely days?

A bird cooed somewhere deeper in the woods and Belle's gaze darted to the shadowy canopy that grew darker with every passing minute.

"Maddie told me your name is Belle." More words from the woman who couldn't be much older than Belle. She wasn't really paying attention to Belle, she was helping Jason as he cut away the injured man's pants and inspected the wound.

Jason's eyes flicked to Belle and back to his task. He hadn't trusted her from the beginning. She didn't blame him. He was kind enough. Doted on his new wife and the three children they'd taken on when the kids' mother and father had passed. But all it took was the right motivation, or a fight, or a bottle. Jason was flesh and blood like the rest. He might betray Maddie one day. Belle would never let her guard down.

"Maddie said you don't have any family?"

The words touched on an old wound. Belle knew the other woman was trying to make a simple conversation but couldn't help the way her head jerked when she shook it.

How old had she been the first time a customer had made her promises? Sixteen? *I wanna marry you. We can be a family.*

Lies. All of them. She'd been naive enough to believe those lies once. Never again.

Men didn't want marriage with a woman like her.

The injured man groaned as Jason probed his wound and Belle's gaze landed on the blood seeping from his broken skin.

Memories instantly overpowered her as her breath caught in her chest. *She was back in that lean-to, a scream trapped in her throat as blood dripped from the end of Sarge's knife, falling silently to the ground.*

And Pretty, sprawled on the ground at his feet.

There was no mistaking the spill of blonde curls—Pretty was the only young woman at the bordello with hair that color.

Even though his back was to her, Belle knew it was Sarge by the scar on the back of his left hand, the midnight-black tangle of hair beneath his hat. Belle pushed the knuckles of her right hand against her trembling mouth, trying to stem the urge to cry out.

He'd killed Pretty. She knew it. A person couldn't lose that much blood and still be alive.

Sarge was pure evil. The older girls had tried to protect Belle from him. It hadn't worked, at least, not all the time. Belle had a scar under the left side of her ribcage from a cut he'd given her with his knife. Other bruises had faded.

Once, he'd nearly choked Sunny to death when he'd been in her room.

And Thaddeus would never do anything about it. Because Sarge brought new customers to the bordello all the time. New cash to line Thaddeus's pockets.

In the flickering light, Sarge's head turned so that she saw his profile. Listening.

She held her breath, frozen, but didn't dare close her eyes.

If he knew she'd witnessed him murder Pretty in cold blood, he'd kill her too. She knew it.

He stood there for far too many heartbeats—until Belle felt the edges of her vision grow dark from holding her breath. And then he wiped the blood from his knife on his pant leg, casual as could be. Walked off into the dark, toward the officer barracks at the nearby fort.

Belle let loose the breath she'd been holding and a soft sob broke loose.

She wanted to scream.

Had she screamed?

Belle blinked back to awareness as the sound came again. A

woman's scream in the distance broke the silence as the last vestiges of light faded into complete darkness.

Coop went on alert, one hand moving to the weapon at his hip as he moved off from the tree he'd been leaning on.

The older brother twirled in a slow circle, eyebrows drawn, an intent expression on his face.

The doc and Alice shared a quick, concerned look.

"You hear that?" the injured man mumbled, words barely audible.

"That sounded human," Coop said.

Belle clutched the knife so tight that it pressed into her palm painfully.

"I don't think it came from the company," Leo said slowly. "It was more to the south." He cut a glance at his brother. "Let's mount up and track her down."

Belle shook her head, but she didn't quite know what she was refusing. The man named Coop was nothing to her.

But he'd saved her once from Sarge.

Coop's gaze shifted to her. And held. She dropped her eyes, still feeling his gaze almost like a physical touch.

"I'm not leaving," Coop said, a stubborn note to his voice.

"He's still out there," she whispered.

Alice's head came up briefly, but maybe no one else heard Belle's words.

Coop kept his hand on the butt of his revolver. "Belle thinks the man who was hunting her might still be out there somewhere. Maybe that was him."

A skeptical expression crossed the older brother's face. But he didn't know—couldn't—how evil Sarge truly was.

"I'm not leaving her," Coop said.

She saw the sideways glance Alice sent to her brother. Caught the hint of judgment in it.

He had family who cared about him. Belle was no stranger to the judgment good folks cast on her. She'd felt it whenever she and Pretty, or one of the other girls, had gone to the fort to shop at the mercantile. Good folks looked down on her. And for good reason.

Belle wasn't like them. She wore a black mark on her—invisible, but still there—and had since she was fourteen and all alone in the wilderness with no money, no family, no future.

Maybe she'd survived, but it was clear she was damaged goods.

"It's dark," Alice called out to her older brother. "What if that was a wild animal?"

The sound came again, a wavering, high-pitched scream. Terrifying enough to send Belle's heart into her throat.

The older brother looked grim. "If someone's in trouble out there, we should go help. C'mon, Coop."

The younger man argued, but Belle didn't register the words as she replayed the older brother's statement in her mind. *"We should go help."*

No one had come to help her. Not any of the good people who had come through the fort. Not any of the men who claimed they loved her.

Whoever that woman was out there in the dark in this godforsaken wilderness, Belle hoped she had a gun or a knife, hoped she knew how to fight.

Because chances were, no one was coming.

Belle clutched her knife tighter as the moon slipped behind a cloud.

Three

"MMPH."

Alice glanced over at the wordless groan from Rob, who lay flat on his back on a litter hastily constructed by Leo and Jason just before dawn.

It couldn't be comfortable. Small branches had been woven together and fastened between two long poles. These poles were connected to the saddle of Jason's horse, the litter carefully dragged behind the animal.

Rob was tied to the litter at his waist and shoulders, and his broken leg was further tied to the one long pole behind it in an effort to steady the broken limb. Rob had been fading in and out of consciousness, still battling the fever trying to rid his body of infection.

Alice worried his groan meant he'd woken again. The last time he'd been awake, she'd noticed his white-knuckled grip on the pole at his side.

Right now, his face remained drawn in sleep, eyes closed.

Maybe it was a blessing. Even though the horse was only moving at a walk, every bump and rock jostled the litter. Rob hadn't complained of the pain once, but Alice knew it must be nigh unbearable.

Jason had pushed for another day of rest out in the wild. Leo had refused, arguing in low, angry tones.

Jason's worry for Rob was clear, even after setting the leg and splinting it tightly, cleaning and stitching the wound.

Alice's worry echoed Jason's. Part of her that wished her heart was more hardened toward Rob. All of this would be easier if she had no memories of his softer side, of warm moments spent together.

It had been an early start for the six of them, and a long day of walking. Evening would fall soon—it'd been almost twenty-four hours since Alice and Jason and Leo had found the others. Leo, riding horseback a few paces ahead, showed no signs of slowing. An hour ago he'd told the group they'd rejoined the same trail the wagons were using. Dark circles shadowed Leo's eyes. He hadn't slept since they'd ridden out yesterday.

Alice remembered the scream that had pierced the night, how Leo had crashed into the darkness searching for whoever had made that sound. He'd returned hours later, empty-handed, frustrated and on edge.

Belle rode a horse Alice didn't recognize—Coop had told her it belonged to the man who'd shot at them and then fell into the gorge. Duncan, Stella's horse, was tied off to this one's saddle. And Coop took up the rear, riding behind where Alice and Jason walked, flanking the litter.

Leo, in no particular hurry, made a wide circle around the horses and litter to come alongside Coop.

Alice let her steps lag, hoping to overhear her older brother say they were going to stop. She was used to walking after this long on the trail, but Leo had pushed for a fast pace today in hopes of catching up to the rest of the company.

"I want to keep going," Leo said instead. "We'll need a couple of torches to light our way. Can you make them?"

Coop pulled a face. "We should stop. Everyone's tired." He jerked his chin toward Alice. Or maybe toward Belle, huddled in her saddle like a shadow.

"We'll catch up faster if we keep going," Leo said, voice level. "Hollis won't push the oxen too hard coming off of this pass. We'll be safer once we reach the caravan."

Alice had slowed enough that she was only a few steps in front of the brothers' horses. "Maybe Coop's right," she offered. "I'm certain R—Mr. Braddock is in some discomfort riding on that litter like he is."

She saw Coop's scowl, quickly hidden in a turn of his head.

Leo glanced over Alice's head and then back to his siblings, frown deepening. "We rode out here to find Coop—and we did —but maybe you two are forgetting that Collin's the only one back with the company to look after the interests of our family."

Alice's stomach pitched at the reminder.

"And he's got an injured wife to look after," Leo pushed. "Don't you care about your own brother?"

"Course I care!" Coop spat.

"Leo—" Alice started.

But her older brother only sent her a quelling hand motion and pointed a scathing look in Coop's direction.

"If you care about this family, prove it. You ran off into the woods without a thought—"

"I *thought* we'd reach the company sooner—"

"Leo—"

Alice was cut off again as Coop made a frustrated noise.

"You never listen to me," her younger brother said.

"When you say something worth listening to, I will."

Stung by Leo's dismissal of Coop, by his refusal to listen to her, Alice picked up her pace to move back beside the litter. She ignored the sideways glance from Jason—who had obviously heard everything her brothers had said—and worked to focus her eyes ahead.

She knew Leo was worried about Evangeline and little Sarah. His wife had a significant dowry that had been left behind by her father, who'd passed early on in the journey. Collin's wife, Stella, had been badly injured, and Collin was taking it hard. And there were the cattle—the livelihood Leo had promised their family once they reached Oregon. Hired cowboys could look after them, but Leo felt a personal responsibility. A weight on him.

But it still stung how he was acting.

The litter shifted as they hit a patch of uneven ground and Alice reached out to steady it, afraid the jerky movement would cause Rob more pain.

He was awake, eyes clear as her hand brushed his shoulder. "You all right?" he asked, voice low.

For one moment, the inadvertent touch and the concern in his voice took her back to the ballroom in his grandfather's mansion. To the one dance they'd shared together, a brief touch of his hand at her lower back, the way his eyes had watched her with such intent promise...

She blinked herself into reality, avoiding Rob's question with a forced smile. "How are you feeling? We've been going for hours..."

His eyes narrowed minutely, as if he'd noticed her redirection, but he said, "Fine and dandy." She could tell his jaw was clenched as he barely let the words escape. "Reckon I'll be up and dancing in no time."

Had he been thinking about that night, too? About what had followed after their shared dance...?

Leo and Coop were still arguing, and a hot flame of embarrassment licked Alice's cheeks.

"Perhaps a little food would keep our spirits up," she said, with forced lightness. "Are you hungry?"

"Not really," Rob muttered, eyes already sliding closed again.

Alice exchanged a look with the doctor. They hadn't brought much in the way of food, only a few dried out biscuits in their saddlebags. Coop and Belle had scarfed down their portion this morning, but Rob hadn't had an appetite all day. What little he'd eaten had come back up not long after. But Alice felt she had to try something.

She hurried forward to the horse they were using as a pack animal, then passed out the remainder of the biscuits to Belle and Jason before slowing so her brothers could catch up.

"I'll make the torches myself—"

Coop interrupted Leo's words by throwing his leg over the horse's back and dismounting quickly. "I never said I wouldn't do it."

"Here," Alice said forcefully. "You both need to eat."

She handed a biscuit to Coop, who snatched it without a thank you, and then she moved to Leo's side, where he still sat in the saddle.

He also didn't offer any appreciation, but she tried not to take it personally.

He stared at Coop, expression hard. "You don't seem to realize the trouble you've landed in. He saved your life." Exhausted from the long night and day, it took Alice a moment to register his pointed finger, aimed right at Rob.

"You think I don't know that?" Coop scoffed. "I pay my debts. I'll help with his oxen and wagon while he's injured."

"You think that'll be enough to pay a life debt?" Leo demanded.

In the gathering dusk, Alice saw color bleed into Coop's cheeks. "I'm good for it—whatever it takes."

Leo's eyes glittered, a hard light deep inside. He lowered his voice. "Braddock is the only man west of the Mississippi who knows about what happened in New Jersey. Knows enough to start rumors. Make your life miserable."

Rob wouldn't— Alice cut off the thought. Maybe at one time she'd thought Rob compassionate. But Coop's mistake had been too big—cost too much.

"What do you want me to do?" Coop demanded.

It was only then she realized how the others had outpaced them. Maybe that was for the best.

"Do you want me to sign my life over? Live as his indentured servant?"

Life debt. Servant.

The words hit hard in light of Alice's former role in the Braddock household.

"You can't," she said. The words seemed to surprise Leo and Coop as much as they did Alice—she hadn't meant to speak them. But more truth spilled out. "The two of you are like flint and steel. You might kill each other if you get too close."

She would never forget the fistfights Coop and Rob had gotten into along this journey. She had to blink against the memory of Coop pummeling Rob, the bruises both Rob and her brother had worn for a week.

Coop wasn't made to be a servant. He had too much spirit to perform a lowly job—even the same ones Alice had performed hundreds of times in the Braddock household. Cleaning food waste, soiled sheets, chamber pots.

Alice had borne it all for years in order to earn money for their household. To keep the family together.

"I'll take on the debt," she blurted.

Leo looked aghast, and Coop wouldn't look at her at all. His focus was on the trail ahead.

Rob would need care so his leg could heal. It would be terrible to be near him, with the past between them, knowing what they'd shared and could never have. But Alice had endured worse. She could bear this, for the sake of her brother.

She had to.

* * *

One. Two. Three. Four. Five.

August Mason counted his steps carefully. It had been weeks since his vision had been stolen by an accident-caused gunpowder explosion, and he'd discovered that counting his steps was one small way he could be independent. Thirty steps from the wagon to where the oxen had been ground tied last night. His brother Owen had helped with that task.

This morning, August was determined to hitch the oxen himself.

His boot caught on a large stone and he nearly lost his balance. He stood for a moment, trying to steady his breath.

He hated this.

He'd always felt he used more than just his sense of sight when he was outdoors, when he was tracking game or scouting for the wagon train. He listened for clues, scented the air, felt the change in the breeze on his skin. But losing his sight had shown him how reliant he was on his eyes. He was nothing without his sight.

He'd held out hope for days after the accident. Prayed that the shadows and hints of light that had come back from the complete darkness would resolve into his natural sight.

But the days had worn on. His constant headache had faded and then gone.

And this was what he was left with. Only a sense of blurred shapes, shadows and near-darkness.

A red bird's call trilled through the woods nearby. *Wee tee. Wee tee.* He could picture the bright red feathers and orange beak, a flash through the greens and browns of the woods.

What else was he missing from this clearing? A doe, tiptoeing through the distant tree trunks? Tracks or scat from a bear?

He'd spent almost three months scouting for Hollis's

company. Was there anyone else capable? Someone who might notice the things August would?

Only last week, the company had been split because of a group of mercenaries. Stella had nearly died. Others had been injured.

If August had been whole, could he have spotted the danger? Protected the company?

He couldn't stand feeling helpless.

There wasn't any use dwelling on his misery.

He started counting again. Fourteen. Fifteen.

He'd taken thirty-three strides when he sensed the first ox near. Had he miscounted because of his stumble? Or perhaps he'd been mistaken last night.

He paused to get his bearings. Could smell the scent of animal hide and manure. Straining his ears, he could hear the ox take a step, crushing sparse grass beneath his hoof.

He gave a few gentle clicks of his tongue as he approached. After all these weeks on the trail, the oxen knew him. But this was the first time August had come to them alone after his injury.

The oxen shied away from August's outstretched hand. He felt the sting of it. He'd always had a way with animals. Now the oxen sensed something was wrong in him, too.

"It's all right," he said, voice low and as calm as he could make it.

He took a step closer, and this time the ox didn't retreat. Its prickly hide flickered at August's touch.

His missing sight had stolen everything from him. Even the ox seemed taller than before.

August ran his hands over the animal's back, followed it as

it side-stepped once. Then he ran both hands down the ox's leg. It was important to check the animals on a long journey like this. Other pioneers' oxen had suffered thrush or injuries to their hooves and legs. August had prided himself on caring for his animals up until now.

The ox let out a sudden bellow—at the same moment a man's shout rang from nearby.

"Get away from my ox!"

Both unexpected noises caught August off guard. He was a half-step too slow when the ox swung its head toward him. August caught the ox's wide, hard skull in the midsection and was thrown backward, landing hard in a sprawl, his hip taking the brunt of the fall.

"August!" Felicity's voice. Instant heat swept over him from head to toe as he realized his wife had witnessed this new humiliation.

With his palms against the ground, he felt the vibration. The ox was charging—

August wrapped both arms over his head and rolled away, praying for protection.

He sensed motion both in front of him and behind.

Someone had intercepted the ox.

Then Felicity's sweet scent enveloped him, air stirred by her skirts as her soft hand touched his shoulder and knelt beside him.

"What were you trying to do?" she whispered urgently.

"You Masons and Spencers think you can interfere with my animals?" A man's voice rang out, fury in his tone.

Who was it? August recognized the voice, almost, but the man's face eluded him.

"Mr. Tanger," Felicity whispered.

August pushed himself up off the ground, shaking off her hand when she tried to support under his elbow.

"I meant to hitch my oxen," August said. He didn't want Felicity's help, or Mr. Tanger's.

"Those aren't our oxen," Felicity whispered urgently.

"Just because your brother is one of the captains....put my family's lives in danger..." Mr. Tanger blustered angrily as August's mind struggled to catch up.

Not his oxen?

"Ours are tied up about fifteen paces to the south," Felicity murmured.

To the south?

He wheeled on his heel, then felt her hand on his arm, stopping him. Pointing him in an entirely different direction.

He knew he'd set off from the wagon in the right direction. How had he managed to end up so far away from where he'd intended to go?

Hot shame sliced through him, anger following quickly on its heels.

"I'm really sorry, Mr. Tanger," Felicity's voice sounded from behind him. "He didn't mean any harm."

August started walking, counting under his breath.

She was apologizing for him. He should be the one apologizing, but couldn't force himself to it.

"Felicity! August!" Ben's voice rang out, with the sound of running footsteps approaching just after.

"This way," the girl directed him with a tug on his arm. Her next statement encompassed them both, so Felicity must be following behind August. "I can't find Whiskers. She's not anywhere in the wagon. She didn't drink her milk this morning."

August sensed a stifled movement from Felicity, just behind and to his right. Ben's kitten had been more trouble than it was worth. It was a curious thing, and this was the second time it'd run off in the past few days.

"Everything all right?" Owen's voice, calling out from a distance. Twenty feet? Thirty? August couldn't judge.

Neither female replied from beside him, but he had the sense of air moving. Had Felicity made some motion to Owen? His brother didn't say anything further.

Another thing to hate. They were communicating without him knowing. More heat stirring the embers of his temper.

"I'll help you look for Whiskers after August and I hitch the oxen," Felicity said. "You run over to Alex and Paul and see if they'll help you look for now."

"All right." Ben was gone as quickly as she'd come, her footsteps fading.

And August had lost count again. Fire raced through his veins as Felicity tugged him to a stop. "The pin is three steps ahead of you."

"I don't want your help," he told her stiffly. "Go and help Ben."

Felicity went perfectly still beside him. "Maybe you don't want my help, August, but you need it."

Her softly spoken words knifed through what was left of his tattered pride.

"You're busy enough managing the wagon and our food and everything else," he argued. "You can't do it all."

"I'm not!" she burst out. He'd only heard this kind of anger in her tone once before. "I'm leaning on our family for help. Like you should be."

"I don't need their charity," he gritted out. "I'm not a cripple or an invalid."

"No one accused you of being so," she snapped. "But you're still getting adjusted to your limitations."

"Limitations?!" he roared. He sensed her take a step back, realized that perhaps he'd frightened her. But he couldn't seem to stop himself now that the mess of emotion inside of him had boiled to an explosion. "I'm half a man, Felicity. Less than that. If I can't start proving my worth, showing that I can take care of myself and my family, then I'm nothing."

It was the first time he'd said it aloud, and the words dropped like stones in a still pool.

There was a moment of quiet. When she spoke, her voice trembled. "That's not true."

"It is true, and we both know it."

This is what he'd kept inside for all these weeks. The truth of it.

"You and Ben would be better off without me."

Four

ROB WOKE to a flare of pain shooting down his leg and up his spine.

At least, he thought he was awake. His eyes were open, but disorientation and the intensity of his pain meant it took long moments for him to realize he was lying on a pallet in the shelter of a wagon. The space inside had been cleared by pushing all the crates and barrels to the front and one side of the wagon. Some kind of linens hung from the bows overhead.

Everything was dark and still. It must be the middle of the night. There were no voices within the wagon train—he'd been dragged into camp on that litter through a haze of pain. Was that yesterday? Or had it been longer than that?

His leg felt like it was on fire. Had the infection returned? Was he going to lose his leg?

His throat felt like a parched desert and he'd sweated through his shirt. He threw off the blanket to his waist and cool air swept in, the damp fabric of his shirt sending goose-bumps over his skin.

Something moved in the darkness outside the wagon. He opened his mouth to call out. Meant to plead for water. But all that emerged was a faint groan.

It didn't matter because the wagon's canvas cover rustled and the flap was pulled back.

More cool air rushed in. Through the opening, he could see a dusting of stars in the sky.

A head and shoulders appeared. The wagon creaked slightly and tipped as the person climbed inside.

"You awake?"

Alice. He'd know that voice anywhere.

How could I care for a man my brothers hate? Her words from days ago rattled through his brain.

"Water?" he rasped. She moved slowly. So slowly.

And then he realized she was doing everything she could not to bump against him, not to rock the wagon.

She settled near his shoulder and he heard the slosh of water.

One of her hands came behind his neck to support him while the other held the tin dipper to his lips.

The water hit his tongue, cold and refreshing. But the fire in his leg didn't abate. He gulped several swallows before she moved the tin cup away.

Her hand that had supported his neck moved slightly, so that her palm was against his scruffy jaw. He craved her touch. He couldn't help himself. He turned his face into her open palm.

Only for her to jerk away.

He wished he could make out her expression, but she was a darker shadow in the darkness inside the wagon. She was quiet —was she even breathing?

He tried to shift his shoulders, but even that movement sent a wave of pain crashing through him. He must've made a noise— one he couldn't hear over the roaring in his head— because she murmured, "Maddie brewed some willow bark tea. It's supposed to help with the pain, if you can keep it down."

"Anything." Had that been his voice, that bare whimper?

She moved to the end of the wagon. Something rustled. The sound of a pour. And then she was back, lifting a tin cup to his lips again.

He took a sip. Choked a little. She moved the cup back.

"That's awful," he breathed. But he choked down several slugs of the bitter liquid anyway.

She put away the cup as he laid flat on his back, the pain blipping through him in waves that seemed to follow his pulse. At least she wasn't leaving.

He fisted his hands into the blankets at his waist when what he really wanted was to hold onto her.

He needed a distraction. Spoke the words before he'd really thought them through. "I thought it would be your brother pouring rank tea down my throat."

She didn't answer. A wave of heat washed through him, making more sweat pop out on his upper lip. He tightened his grip on the blanket.

"You never should've followed me on this journey." Her soft words seemed to come from the darkness itself.

"Who else was going to watch over you?" He couldn't seem

to hide the desperate, pained note from his voice. Prayed she wouldn't hear it.

"My brothers," came her matter-of-fact answer.

"You mean Leo, too wrapped up in his new wife and child to notice when you're frustrated with Coop? Or Collin, too sick to ride with you to the fort?"

Rob had ridden with her. Had noticed her stricken expression more than once when she'd finished dealing with Coop.

She was quiet. For far too long. Maybe the fever was making him hallucinate again, but he would've sworn he could feel hurt radiating off of her.

And the last thing he wanted to do was hurt her.

He'd let go of the blanket at some point and now scrabbled to grip it again as his leg spasmed and pain shot through him. He bumped the toe of her boot. Tried to breathe through the pain.

"I would've chased after you anyway." He gritted out the words. "Regardless if your brothers were here or stood in my way."

She remained quiet, but this time he sensed that she was listening.

"I figure it was my fault," he said quietly. "I scared you off. I pushed for too much, too quickly. I should've courted you like a lady."

"I'm not a lady," she argued.

For a second, his memories of the night of the ball played through his mind. Alice like he'd never seen her before. Wearing the pale blue dress he'd paid a fine penny for at the most expensive seamstress in town. Her hair pulled behind her head and soft strands framing her face. He'd felt himself falling in love with her as they'd danced in the crowded ballroom. Every pass, every slide of his hand against hers in the movements of the dance... he'd wanted to sweep her into his arms and carry her off to a preacher. Claim her as his bride, keep her forever at his side.

He should've followed the impulse.

But life had gotten in the way. Things had gotten messy.

"We're too different," she said now, breaking him from those thoughts. "It never would've worked between us."

She'd said as much before. He didn't believe it. Not with the way she'd looked at him the night of the ball. She'd felt it, too.

"It *will* work between us," he countered. "We make a fine match."

"You're speaking nonsense—" she muttered.

"Fannie would've come around."

"Fever," she murmured when he mentioned his cousin.

Not Grandfather, though. The thought flew in and back out of Rob's consciousness so quickly he barely registered it. He'd left a letter at home explaining his decision to come West. The reasoning behind starting a sawmill in Oregon, where folks would need lumber. Rob had known Grandfather would have a hundred reasons he shouldn't come.

And that's exactly why Rob had needed to leave.

So he'd gone like a thief in the night. Grandfather would rage, threaten, try to control the situation from thousands of miles away. But by the time Rob was established and sent word home, it would be too late. Grandfather would have to accept that Rob had built something on his own terms. Proved he didn't need the Braddock name to succeed.

He must've drifted off.

He came to again, his pain slightly less, but he was shivering so badly that it wracked his entire body.

"What's the matter?" Alice, her voice disembodied in the darkness. She pulled the blanket up around his shoulders.

"Jus' cold." He slurred his words a little. Maybe she wouldn't speak to him tomorrow. He couldn't know. But if this was his one chance, he wasn't going to waste it.

"I knew the first moment I saw you in that green dress. In the upstairs hallway."

A pause. And when she spoke, resignation in her voice. "You saw me for years before that. You simply never noticed."

"It's my biggest regret."

She didn't respond to his admission. His shivers got worse, until his quivering created a new shaft of pain down his leg.

She touched his shoulder. Maybe to ensure he was still wrapped in the blanket? Or to steady him.

He heard her voice as if from far away. "I can wake Leo. Move you close to the fire."

"I'll be fine." But his teeth were chattering.

He thought she would leave. But after a broken moment, she laid down in the narrow space next to him, wrapped one arm around his waist as she rested her head on his shoulder.

It wasn't improper—how could it be, when they were both fully clothed and there was a blanket between them? And it felt right to have her curled up beside him. Like everything in the universe had aligned to give him what he'd dreamed of.

They were meant to be together.

Tendrils of warmth crept through him as she stayed, her breath soft on his jaw.

She didn't believe it yet. That they were meant to be. She had an argument for everything he'd said tonight.

What could he do to convince her?

The first thing he needed to do was get well. Then he could prove to her that they were a perfect match.

He *would* win her back.

* * *

"There's enough for one more cup of coffee." Alice extended the coffeepot with her brows raised in invitation.

Doc looked up from where he knelt beside Rob and shook his head.

Leo had helped Rob hobble into the woods for morning ablutions and the stubborn man had asked to sit by the fireside to eat breakfast. He'd looked nearly green but forced down a pan biscuit and a few bites of venison steak.

Now he sat still through Doc's prodding, face white and expression shuttered. In pain.

Coop and Collin were nearby, saddling up a pair of horses. Close enough for Alice to catch snatches of their conversation.

"Hollis wants us off this mountain as soon as can be." Collin sent a worried glance at Stella's wagon. His wife was restless enough as it was. Riding in a wagon—injured—at a fast pace down this rough terrain wouldn't be easy on her.

Coop seemed to be barely paying attention. His hands hovered beneath his saddle, ostensibly fastening the cinch around the horse's middle, but his gaze rested on a wagon across the clearing.

Alice looked that direction and realized it wasn't a wagon

that had arrested her brother's attention at all. It was Belle, perched on a crate beside the wheel of Maddie and Doc's wagon, young Alex chatting at her.

Alice hummed an old tune Mama had taught her as she scooped up the pile of clean plates she'd rinsed off in the icy creek water earlier then moved toward Leo's wagon to put them away. The air had taken on a sharp, biting quality that made her breath visible in small puffs. She glanced up at the gray sky—the clouds hung low and heavy, pregnant with the promise of snow. Alice always added her own flourishes to the melody, making it her own. It was one of the few times she felt truly herself—when the notes rose from somewhere deep inside and she could shape them into something beautiful, even if no one was listening.

"There's another mountain range ahead, isn't there?" Coop asked.

Alice's spirits fell a little as she leaned into the wagon to put the dishes in their crate. She'd hoped the company was close to the end of this journey. Days on end of cooking over an open fire wore on a body. There wasn't much time for laundering clothes or bedding—and sometimes there wasn't enough water to do so.

She wanted to be back in a home. A house. With walls, not wheels.

She glanced over her shoulder again. Coop was still mooning over Belle, distracted from the words Collin was saying to him, too low for Alice to catch.

She glanced back at Belle. Out in the wild, Alice had been so involved with helping reset Rob's leg and keeping the fire going that she'd barely interacted with the young woman. Belle seemed skittish and withdrawn. What could Coop possibly see in her? Was he only attracted to her because of her profession? Did he see her as someone easy to approach?

As Alice watched, a man and his teenaged daughter walked past Doc's campsite. The man stared at Belle—no, he was leering at her.

Alice shivered as she watched Belle wrap her tattered shawl more tightly around her shoulders and turn her head away. Alex didn't seem to notice the interaction. A moment later, the man was gone.

Alice glanced back at Coop. He must've seen the whole thing, for he was two steps away from his horse, only turning back to Collin's insistent voice after a long look at Belle.

Alice went back to the dying fire for the coffeepot. "What is he thinking?" She muttered the words under her breath, but Doc must've heard anyway.

He was far too observant, because even without glancing up he knew that Alice's concern was Belle and how distracted Coop was by the young woman.

Doc shook his head slightly. "I didn't agree with Maddie harboring a stowaway at first. We had words."

Alice stifled a smile as she moved the coffeepot away from the fire and then used a bucket of water to douse the remaining embers. The fire spit and steam and smoke wafted into the air. It was a well-known fact that Doc and Maddie had crossed swords numerous times before they'd made peace with each other—and fallen in love.

"Now there's no hiding her presence," Doc went on. "I can only hope having her as part of the company won't cause any issues."

Was he talking about Coop directly? Or what other men might think or want? Or jealous wives?

Alice frowned at the last of the ashes, now cold mush.

Rob had his eyes closed and face turned away in pain as Doc replaced his bandage.

When Doc straightened to his full height, he tucked something in his black doctor's bag. "Not all women choose the life she was mired in," he said quietly. "Maddie has pried and waited and Belle's only told her bits and pieces of it—but for a young girl to be forced to do what she's had to in order to survive..." He shook his head, a muscle in his jaw jumping.

Shock and dismay battled inside Alice as realization settled on her. Belle couldn't be more than seventeen or eighteen. Was Doc speaking true? If she'd been forced into life at a bordello as a teenager—

"How awful," Alice breathed. Suddenly convicted of how harshly she'd judged the other woman, Alice pressed a fist to her chest.

In the distance, the bugle blew a warning. The company would begin to pull out in a few minutes.

"I've got to check on Mrs. Browning before we start moving." Doc threw a glance over his shoulder at Rob.

"I'll help him into the wagon if Leo doesn't come back by," she said quickly.

Doc was off with only a nod for a goodbye.

Alice only had a moment. She grabbed a tin cup and rushed to where Coop was swinging into the saddle. Collin had already gone.

"I've got one last cup of coffee," she offered as she held it up to him.

He thanked her with a nod and brought the cup to his lips. Over the rim, his eyes still went in the direction of Maddie's wagon, though Belle was now gone.

Alice had intended to caution him off of his interest in Belle, but Doc's revelation had confused things. And maybe that wasn't the most urgent matter right now.

"How are you feeling this morning?" she asked instead.

When he shrugged, she went on. "I was really worried about you, being out there alone. Leo was too."

He pulled a face as he put the now-empty coffee cup back in her hand. "I'll wager he wasn't."

Coop was too stubborn to recognize how much Leo worried over him. Loved him.

"Can't you try to get along?" she asked. "For me?"

Her brother scowled. "Why don't you ask him? Why's it on me?"

"It's not—"

"Leave off, Alice." He nudged the horse into motion, ending the conversation before she was ready.

He galloped away, toward where the cowboys had stayed with the cattle overnight. She'd said the wrong thing.

Again.

Shame licked heat into her face as she passed by the wagon, depositing the cup inside before moving to Rob's side.

She couldn't meet his stare. Of course he'd heard the whole thing.

A glance around showed everyone stowing the last of their camp items or guiding oxen into the line of departing wagons. It was time to go. And Leo was nowhere to be seen.

She moved to Rob's side, carefully avoiding his injured leg, and slipped her shoulder beneath his arm and into his side so she could help him lever to his feet.

"You all right?"

She felt the rumble of his voice where their sides touched. Tried not to feel anything.

"Of course." She aimed the false smile at him, but didn't give him her eyes.

"You don't look all right."

Why could the stubborn man not leave it alone?

"I suppose I lost some sleep last night," she grumbled, trying to put a bit of teasing into her voice. Distract him from what he'd witnessed between her and Coop.

She helped him hobble a few steps toward the wagon, felt the change in his breathing as it became more labored.

"I can't be sorry about that," he said.

She flushed, remembering the way she'd curled up to his shivering body. She'd only meant to share her body heat with him for a few minutes and then leave. But with her cheek pillowed on his shoulder, his arm curling around her, she'd felt—

She cut that thought off.

Only for it to be replaced by the memory of his fingers feathering into her hair as he'd drifted off to sleep.

She stumbled the last step to the wagon, steadied herself with a hand against the sideboard and hoped he wouldn't notice how discomfited she'd become.

It took the two of them some doing to get him up into the wagon bed and then backwards into the narrow space where he'd spend the day. By the time they were finished, he was sweating and trembling.

"I'll be driving the oxen," she said, breathing hard and thankful for the chance to back out of the wagon. "I won't be far if you need anything."

His stare followed her out of the wagon. "Why isn't Coop the one taking care of me?"

He saw too much.

She lifted her chin as she answered. "The only thing that matters to me is bringing Coop back into the fold of this family. That won't happen if Coop is fighting with you the rest of the way to the Willamette Valley."

There was a sharpness in his gaze as he watched her.

She tried to inject some levity into the moment strung tight with tension. "Besides, I'm used to waiting on your family. I've done it for years."

"And if I don't want you to?" Something colored his tone she couldn't make out. Not anger. Something else.

She firmed her lips. "I'll do anything to keep my family together. Family is the only thing that matters."

But as she walked away from the wagon's opening, moving toward the oxen to call for them to move out, she pressed her hand against her midsection. Being close to Rob last night and again just now made her tender insides feel shredded into tatters.

How long could she keep this up?

Five

"YOU CAN'T CATCH ME!"

"Hurry, Ben! This way!"

Alice panted as she chased little Sarah along the map of lines Alice had painstakingly drawn into the sandy ground earlier. The cool afternoon air nipped at her cheeks, and she was grateful for the exertion that kept her warm.

"Watch out!"

"The fox is coming!"

Ben and Alex shrieked as they ran along the outer rim of the big circle drawn on the ground.

Paul motioned to Jenny, who was too little to understand the rules of the game and was toddling her way all over the course, mostly following her brothers with a gleeful, gummy smile.

Alice came up behind Sarah, who shrieked happily as Alice scooped the tot into her arms with a pretend, ferocious growl.

She smacked a loud kiss on her niece's chubby cheek and put the girl back on the ground.

Panting, Alice gave chase to the other children, who scattered in all directions on the course. Alex's dog Tommy barked and ran after Ben.

It was late in the afternoon. Hollis had called for an early halt after the company had come out of the Rocky Mountains and into the foothills. Rob sat propped against one of the wagon wheels nearby, his splinted leg stretched out before him, a blanket draped across his lap. He'd been watching the game with a shuttered expression.

All the pioneers were weary. A few hours of rest or play this afternoon would make for better travel tomorrow.

Over the past two days, Alice had spent hours trying to think of what Mother would've done to make Leo and Coop stop arguing.

It had finally come to her last night as she'd drifted off to sleep. Fox and Goose.

Her brothers had loved the game when they'd been young. They would play for hours, begging for Alice to participate. It was a form of tag, but the Geese had to stay within the lines, drawn like the spokes of a wheel, confined to a larger circle as they tried to reach their "base," an inner circle.

Ma had once confided in a teenaged Alice that when the boys would fight, she would set up the game in the grassy space outside their tiny house and the boys would inevitably make up as they played.

Coop and Leo made the best team.

Alice could almost hear her mother's voice in her memory. Oh, how she missed Mama.

Today, Alice was determined to make her brothers realize how well they worked together—and how much they needed each other.

The men would come to the campsite for supper soon enough. Maddie arrived now, wiping her hands on her apron as she came from the direction of the creek. Alice knew she'd been called away to help a grandmotherly woman who was having some joint pain.

"Maddie! Come play with us!" Alex called out.

Collin rounded one of the wagons. His face lit up when he caught sight of the game. He leaned his head into the wagon, must've said something to Stella, resting inside, and then jogged toward the course.

"Who's the fox?" he demanded.

Maddie laughed as Alex tugged her into the big circle. "You'll have to tell me how to play."

A few minutes later, Leo and Evangeline joined in. Leo put little Sarah on his shoulders, and they took over as the Fox.

Alice couldn't help an awareness of Rob watching her as she took herself out of the game to fetch a dipper of water from the bucket tied off on the side of the wagon.

"You look like you're having fun," he murmured as her quest for water brought her within a few feet of where he was propped against the wagon wheel.

She must have looked a mess. Her cheeks were flushed from the running, and she could feel her hair falling out of its pins. She'd worn this dress nearly every day of this journey—an old work dress from before they'd left Missouri. She averted her eyes as she sipped from the dipper, choosing silence over engaging with him.

The past two days had been torturous. It had been a relief to drive the oxen that pulled his wagon, to have him out of sight and sequestered inside the wagon. But the evenings and the mornings—the times when she had no choice but to see him, to help him—were difficult.

We make a fine match. Rob's words from last night played through her memory.

Why couldn't she forget everything that had passed between them back in New Jersey? Things would be so much easier if she had no memory of his tender smiles, the way he'd protected her, cared for her.

Kissed her.

She didn't want to think about it at all.

She gave him a tight smile. "How's your pain? Would you like some willow bark tea?"

He pulled a face, one that would've made her laugh in another time. "I'd rather not drink that tea ever again, if I can help it. I'm all right."

He wasn't telling the truth. She could see the white lines of pain around his mouth, the stiff way he held himself. And his cheeks were flushed with fever.

She put the dipper back in the water bucket. "Stella was asking for a bath. Evangeline and I will haul up some water after supper. I suppose it would do you good to wash up?"

He gave a sort of grunt in agreement. He hadn't argued with her about whether it should be Alice or Coop helping him since the first time he'd brought it up, but there were times —like when he needed help changing his shirt or moving around—that she had the sense he didn't appreciate it being Alice who witnessed him in pain.

She caught movement in her peripheral vision and realized Coop was striding into camp. Alice excused herself from Rob and rushed over to her brother, now staring at the group of adults and children playing. His expression was shuttered.

"Come and play with us," she pleaded, reaching for his arm with both hands. "It's just like when we were children. Do you remember....?"

"Alice—" He shook his head, but she tugged on his arm. Tipped her head to the side.

"Please? Think of how many times you begged and I gave in, back when we were children."

He groaned a little but gave in to her pleading and followed her to the course.

"Coop's playing, too!" she called out as she neared.

"Maybe I should take a break!" Maddie huffed, only to receive a chorus of "no's" from the children.

"We'll have two new foxes," Alice announced. "Leo and Coop. The best team."

She caught a flash of a smile from Collin. Did he realize what she was trying to do?

Ben darted away from the circle, her braids flying, and ran straight to where August stood at the edge of the gathering. The little girl tugged on his sleeve.

"C'mon August, you should be a fox too!" Ben's voice rang out clear and bright. "You could catch us easy. We're real loud when we run."

August's face softened for just a moment as he looked down toward the sound of her voice. His hand came to rest briefly on the top of her head. But then his expression shuttered.

"I don't think—"

"You could," Alice said, her voice emerging too eager, too hopeful. She took a step toward them. "Ben's right. You only need to follow the sounds. The children make plenty of noise."

August's jaw tightened. His hand dropped from Ben's head. "Leave off, Alice."

The words were quiet but firm. Final.

Ben's face fell. She glanced between August and Alice, confused by the sudden tension.

"But—" the little girl started.

"Go on and play," August said, his tone gentler with the child.

Ben hesitated, then scampered back to the game, casting one last uncertain look over her shoulder.

Alice stood frozen, heat creeping up her neck. She'd only been trying to—

But what did it matter what she'd been trying to do?

August had already turned away, his shoulders rigid as he moved back toward his wagon.

The children shrieked and ran along the spokes of lines in the ground, even as Alice jogged away.

Behind her, Leo uttered a low command to Coop, but she couldn't make out the words. She looked over her shoulder, hoping to see some hint of their brotherly connection.

Leo handed Sarah to Evangeline.

Coop darted off along one of the spokes.

Leo stared after him with a scowl.

Oh no. What had gone wrong?

Leo set off in a different direction, quickly catching Ben and then Maddie.

Coop tagged Alice, then went after Paul. And met Leo just behind the boy, who was trapped between them.

Leo frowned. "I said for you to move clockwise."

Coop shrugged. "I didn't want to."

"You can't listen, even in a simple game!"

As Leo's voice rose, Alice tried to get between the two men.

"Perhaps we should start the round again," she said, a little too brightly.

Coop's expression was closed off. "There's no need. Collin can take my place. I've got to head out. It's my watch with the cattle."

He strode off, ducking through the narrow space between two wagons and disappearing.

The children started calling for a new game even as Leo's frown tightened.

"It wouldn't have hurt for you to play nice—" she started.

"Stay out of it, Alice." Leo's sharp words battered the shred of hope she held on to.

Leo turned his frown on her. "Coop's made it clear he doesn't want to be a part of this family any more."

"He hasn't said any such thing."

"He didn't have to," Leo ground out. "Save your games and energy for other tasks."

Leo stomped off, leaving Alice with tears stinging her eyes.

She stepped backwards, barely avoiding being bowled over by Paul, who was darting along the outer rim of the circle.

Shaky, Alice moved away from the game and toward the fire, where she could put her back to the others, including Rob. Who must've seen everything, even if he might not have overheard Leo's unkind words.

Alice stirred the embers to flames, used a long-handled wooden spoon to lift the lid over the pot and check on the venison stew warming over the fire.

Two women passed by, their voices carrying.

"—told you, one of Johnson's best laying hens is just gone," the first woman said. "Feathers everywhere, but no body."

"Could've been a fox," the second replied.

"That's what Mr. Johnson figures. But the strange thing is, there were these scratches on the coop. Deep ones. Like something big tried to get in."

Their voices faded as they moved past.

Thankfully, Rob stayed silent. Though she could feel his gaze on her.

Movement lifted her head as Doc joined her at the fire. "Collin said you might help Stella bathe tonight?"

Alice nodded. "Is that all right?"

She would be grateful for the distraction of it.

"She's really weak. Fighting off infection in the wound." He sounded worried, and Alice sent a glance over her shoulder to see Collin chasing Ben with a wolf-like howl. Her brother looked so carefree. She was glad for the few moments he wasn't worrying over his wife and unborn baby.

"My stock of disinfectant is running low," Doc confessed, still sounding worried.

"I've got more in my supplies." The unexpected words from Rob had both Alice and Doc's heads turning toward him.

"You can have whatever you need," he offered.

Doc's eyes lit. "Thank you."

But Alice's chest felt tight. "You had medicine in your supplies? During the epidemic?"

Rob's expression grew guarded. "Yes, some."

"Why didn't you share what you had?" she demanded.

He shook his head. "It wasn't the right kind of med—"

Doc nodded. "He's right."

But the spark of temper that Alice was holding wouldn't be doused. Rob had left Missouri with a wagon packed full of supplies that others couldn't afford. It wasn't fair.

Doc watched her. Said in a low voice, "Who do you think bribed those soldiers from the fort to come and help?"

"Bribed?"

Rob looked away as her eyes trained on him. Color rose in his neck and jaw.

Doc wasn't finished. "Hollis asked for help more than once and was refused. I overheard the soldiers claiming someone had paid them to risk their own health to help our company."

A bribe.

Rob could clearly hear the two of them talking and wasn't denying it.

Shaken, she stood and walked away from the fire, past the ring of wagons until the noise faded. She'd foolishly thought *she* had been the reason the soldiers had come to help the company. She and Rob had ridden all night long, through dangerous terrain to reach the fort. She'd begged the sergeant for help. Hadn't noticed that Rob had quietly made a bribe.

Tears rose in her eyes and she closed her eyes against them.

Foolish.

She was so foolish.

She'd thought that her actions had mattered. That what she'd done had been a help. She'd believed she'd saved lives.

But it had been Rob—Rob's money—that had made the difference.

Alice had done nothing.

* * *

Evening was fading as Rob watched Alice haul buckets and more buckets of water from the nearby creek. She and Leo's wife, Evangeline, had created a makeshift "room" by stringing lines between two wagons and draping sheets over them to block anyone from viewing the small tub they'd put inside so Stella could bathe.

He wanted a chance to sit and talk with Alice. A few minutes would assuage the need boiling inside him. But she never seemed to stop working.

If it wasn't hauling water for bath time, it was washing clothes down at the creek. She'd strung clean laundry across a different wire between two wagons across the way. Made supper with help from Evangeline. Darned socks in the few minutes she sat down while waiting on supper to heat. She never stopped.

Rob tracked her movement as she emerged from behind the makeshift bathing room, two empty pails swinging from her hands. She started toward the creek path, then slowed.

August stood near his wagon, his hands moving carefully over the canvas ties, clearly trying to secure them for the night. His fingers fumbled over a knot that had pulled tight. Once. Twice. The third time, his jaw tightened with frustration.

Alice stopped walking entirely.

Rob saw the way her whole body angled toward August.

The way her grip shifted on the pail handles, as if preparing to set them down. Her lips parted, and Rob could almost hear the offer forming: Let me help you with that.

But then something changed.

Her shoulders drew back. Her mouth closed. She turned her face away from August's struggle and started walking again, her steps perhaps a bit quicker than before.

She didn't look back.

Rob watched August work at the stubborn knot for another few moments before Owen appeared from the other side of the wagon to help. But Alice was already gone, disappearing into the dusk toward the creek.

Something about the moment unsettled Rob. He'd seen Alice rush to help everyone—Stella, the children, even strangers in camp who needed assistance. She'd helped him constantly, despite everything between them.

But she'd walked right past August.

When she returned a few minutes later, pails sloshing with water, the lightness that had briefly touched her face during the children's game was gone. Her movements were efficient, mechanical. She set the pails down near the bathing area with more force than necessary, water splashing over the rims.

Her jaw was set in a way that reminded Rob of someone biting back words they couldn't say. Or maybe tears they wouldn't shed.

She caught him watching and quickly looked away, but not before he saw the tightness around her eyes. The same look she'd worn when Leo had dismissed her concerns about Coop. When Coop had told her to stay out of his business.

It was the look of someone who'd been told one too many times that her help wasn't wanted.

Rob had watched her set up and join the game of tag. For a few minutes, before her brothers had gotten involved, she'd lost herself in play. Laughed with the children. Turned her face up to the sky with her eyes closed, enjoying the sunshine on her face.

And then those two scoundrel brothers had to go and ruin her fun. Couldn't they see how hard she worked? As hard as any man, surely.

It made him itch.

He wanted a chance to give Coop Spencer a good walloping. But that would have to wait until Rob healed up.

Rob heard the murmur of female voices, a splash and a soft gasp, saw movement behind those curtains. It had gone dark by the time Alice appeared.

Her skirt was dark where it must've gotten wet while she helped Stella. She sent Rob a tight-lipped look and then picked up two empty pails and started to leave camp.

He wanted to call after her. It was still light out, but growing dark quickly. She didn't need to be out in the woods alone.

She returned in a few minutes. And headed straight toward him. His spirits started to lift, until he registered the pails in her hand.

He'd been lying on the pallet where Leo and Collin had put him after the game but now pushed himself up to a sitting position again.

It took three times as long as it should've, and he was sweating. His leg ached anew, even though he'd tried not to move it at all.

Alice's lips were pursed as she stopped at the edge of his pallet and set down her pails.

"You shouldn't be trying to sit up," she murmured, though her gaze went everywhere but him.

"What's the water for?" he asked.

She wrinkled her nose. "Don't tell me you're in the same camp as young Alex and will refuse a bath when it's offered."

"I'd prefer to wash up on my own."

Her gaze flicked to him and then away. "By all means." She extended one arm toward the woods. "Would you like to walk to the creek on your own?"

Heat flushed his face. She knew he couldn't.

"You're clearly in pain." She touched his forehead, only for a moment, before whisking her hand away. "And feverish. The best thing for you is to sleep, and you can do that after you wash up."

He'd seen her stubbornness first-hand, hadn't he? She'd refused to speak to him for weeks on end as the journey had unfolded. And he was too tired to keep fighting with her now.

"I'll do it," he grumbled, fingers going to the buttons of his shirt. "Just leave the water. And soap. Please."

She pinched her lips together. "I don't like this any more than you do, but—" She inhaled deeply. Closed her eyes for a brief second. "You won't be able to wash your hair. Doc doesn't want you to get any water or dirt in the wound. You'll need to lie back and let me help."

She was right.

He shed his shirt and sponged off his torso, clearing the dirt and accumulated sweat as she disappeared into the darkness after more water. His skin prickled with goosebumps as the cool water evaporated. She was right. He did feel better being clean.

When she returned, her eyes skittered away from his bare chest.

"I've a clean shirt in my wagon," he muttered.

She was back in a few minutes, her jaw locked tight. She hung the shirt on a nearby wagon wheel before coming to kneel by his side.

"Can you lie back?" she asked.

He must've twisted wrong as he attempted it, because white-hot pain fired up his leg and spine. And gasped, because suddenly her cool hand rested against his shoulder, supporting him. Had she rolled the edge of his pallet blanket up? Because suddenly his shoulders were supported and his head up off the ground.

"All right?" she asked tightly.

Still shaky from the pain, he gritted out, "Fine."

Her hand came behind his head, offering support as she poured water into his hair with a tin cup. The cool water was a shock at first, but then felt like a relief against his fevered skin. He closed his eyes against the sensation. Unfortunately, with his eyes closed, there was no avoiding the feeling of her fingers threading through his hair.

"Why are you angry with me?" he asked.

She let go of his head for a moment and his eyes opened. She was lathering soap between her hands. He closed his eyes again.

She gently scrubbed soap into his hair before she finally

answered. "Why didn't you tell me you'd paid the soldiers to come and help during the epidemic?"

He couldn't think of one thing that would compare to the pleasurable sensation of her fingers trailing along his scalp. Not one.

Which made the stiff, almost angry question from her lips so ironic.

"Your knowing wouldn't have made a difference."

Her fingers went still for a moment, and he rushed on, "I wanted to help you."

"Like your money helped Coop out of trouble back in New Jersey?" Her forceful words stood in stark opposition to the gentle scrubbing of her hands.

"If my money can help you, why shouldn't I use it? It makes no matter to me," he argued.

Her fingers left his scalp completely. Now he felt a new drench of water being poured, her fingers brushing through his hair to wash away the soap.

He'd thought—hoped—that Alice would continue the conversation. But she remained silent as she rinsed his hair.

A breath of pause before a warm cloth wrapped around his head. A towel, he realized.

She helped him sit up, slowly, painfully. Wouldn't look at him as she wiped off his shoulders. Handed him his shirt.

He gripped her wrist before she could move away. Her eyes flashed to his.

"Why does it bother you so much?" he demanded, voice low, aware of Stella in that wagon nearby and Evangeline's quiet voice as she sang little Sarah to sleep.

Alice tried to pull away, but he held fast. "Fannie would accept the help as a gift—"

"I'm not your cousin!" Alice's words exploded in the quiet between them. She tugged her hand away but stayed with both hands on her knees, kneeling beside him. She was breathing as if she'd just run across the entire camp.

"The amount of money you paid those men to disperse when they'd bet on Coop's boxing skills was absurd," she said, the words quick and angry. "It would've paid rent for my brothers and me for two months!"

He felt a beat of surprise, but now that she'd started, she wasn't finished.

"Or could've fed the malnourished children in our tenement for weeks." She shook her head. "And you just threw it at Coop's situation as if it was nothing." Her furious gaze landed on him. "You could've done so much good with it."

"I did," he countered evenly. "I used it to help you. And the money I paid for those soldiers to help was meant to benefit everyone in camp."

Her hands fisted on her knees.

He reached out and touched her nearest hand. She jumped, pulling away from his touch.

"Tell me why this matters so much," he demanded softly.

"It doesn't." Her lips firmed. "It only proves that I've been right all along. We're too different, you and I."

"Alice, it's just money—"

Her eyes flashed again, though he thought that sparkle might be from tears she was holding back. "That's what someone would say who has never gone to bed with their stomach gnawing with hunger. Never worried that one mistake would cost them a job—and mean their children wouldn't have a place to live."

Heat climbed up his throat and into his face. "Do you want me to apologize that I was born into the Braddock family? It isn't as if I chose to be born into wealth."

She shook her head. Bit her lip and gave him her profile.

At some point in tonight's efforts, all the work she'd done, the top button of her shirtwaist had come undone. The bit of skin at her throat wasn't inappropriate in the least—but it was the flash of gold at her neck that arrested his attention now. A thin gold chain had slipped free, and a small golden locket dangled there at the base of Alice's throat.

The gold locket he'd gifted her on the night of the ball.

She was speaking, and it took everything in him to focus on her words. "...sometimes people think too differently to ever be able to come to agreement."

There was a tone of resignation in her voice that begged for argument. But he couldn't seem to look away from that locket.

She'd worn it, all this time?

She'd pushed him away. Refused to see him, talk to him. It'd taken this broken leg and him nearly losing his life to the fever to even gain a chance for conversation.

But that locket... it meant that she'd never forgotten what they'd had. Perhaps that she'd never given up, no matter what her words said.

His mind snapped into focus and he lifted his gaze to her face. Saw the flare of surprise at the way his eyes searched her expression.

He couldn't give up now. Not after this sign that there was still something between them.

"Two people don't have to agree in every way to make a marriage work between them," he said quietly.

It was the wrong thing to say. He knew it the moment the words emerged from his mouth. Bringing up marriage when she was barely speaking to him.

She huffed and stood up, left without another word.

He let his head loll back on the blanket, exhausted from the few movements it had taken to wash up, but with new hope lighting in his chest.

Alice wore his locket.

Six

THUNDER ROLLED in the far distance.

Inside the wagon, Rob laid down the stub of pencil he'd been using, his jaw clenching as another wave of pain rolled through his leg. He forced his head back against the crate behind him, breathing through his nose. It was cold enough that he wore a quilt over his legs and had thrown his coat around his shoulders.

The constant hum of pain beneath his skin should've begun to fade by now. The fact that it hadn't—that it pulsed through him like the blade of a knife with every heartbeat— sent a cold thread of worry through his chest. But underneath the worry, anger simmered. His hands fisted against his thighs.

Had the infection spread after Doc had cleaned Rob's wound out in the wild? Or was this simply the way his body felt as it knit together a bone broken so badly? He refused to accept that this was as good as it would get.

It didn't help that the company had been stopped for an hour already.

Rob had fixed a squat piece of candle on a saucer and it threw light in a strange pattern as it flickered.

Another rumble of thunder, this one closer.

Hollis hadn't known what to make of the storm. That's why he'd called for an early halt. Fine snowflakes swirled down from the darkened sky, some of them sneaking inside the place where the canvas covering of Rob's wagon had become loosened by the chill wind. Who had ever heard of a snowstorm with thunder and lightning?

But an occasional bolt of lightning, followed by thunder, created more danger for the wagons.

Rob wanted out of this wagon. That didn't seem likely while the storm raged—and he wouldn't ask Alice to risk herself by going out in it.

The days had grown monotonous as he'd been confined to ride in the back of the wagon. His only relief were the mornings and evenings when Alice helped him down and into camp. Today, he'd managed to prop himself up to a sitting position in the back of the wagon, leaning against a stack of crates. He'd pulled out all of his notes and sketches for the sawmill from the leather pouch where he normally kept them, bound by thin leather cords. Everything was spread out alongside him, some of it sitting on crates he used as his tables. Seeing all of his careful planning made the itch to be up and about worse.

A loud clap of thunder rattled the wagon—and his teeth— and there was a sudden scrabbling at the back of the wagon.

"Hello?" he called out.

No answer, but there was definitely someone fumbling with the ties that held the canvas cover together.

Why hadn't they answered?

"Who is it?" he demanded, more loudly this time.

Still no answer, but the canvas loosened and opened.

He had a wild thought that perhaps he should call for help—would anyone even hear him, if all the other pioneers were tucked in their wagons?—just before a head peeked through.

Sarah. Evangeline's little girl.

"What're you—?"

Another loud crack of thunder. She made a noise of distress before she scrambled through the opening and landed heavily on the wagon bed, narrowly missing his splinted leg.

Fine snowflakes and cold air swirled inside. It had grown even darker outside. He couldn't see much of anything.

"What's wrong?" he asked.

Little Sarah panted, her eyes wide and frightened as she looked around.

How had she come to be out there alone? Where was her mother? Leo?

Lightning flashed. She jumped, crying out.

There was no accompanying roll of thunder, but it didn't seem to help. Two big tears rolled down the girl's cheeks as she glanced at him—clearly frightened of him—and then at the opening.

Rob shifted, the movement sending a spear of pain down his leg. He clenched his jaw to keep from groaning.

Wherever her parents were, they were likely going out of their minds with worry. But he clearly couldn't get out of this wagon without help.

"Anyone out there?" he called out.

The girl shuffled away from him, still frightened.

And when she eyed the opening in the canvas again, he had the terrifying thought that she might try to go back out into the storm. He could barely move. He wouldn't be able to stop her.

He lowered his voice, gentled it. "It's going to be all right. I'm sure your mama will be here in just a minute, looking for you."

She put the thumb of one hand in her mouth, eyes still wide.

Was she too young to speak? He'd seen her laughing with Evangeline, clapping her hands. But he hadn't paid enough attention to know if she could talk.

Inspiration struck. He reached into a small, open crate stacked on two other crates behind his right shoulder. He found the paper-wrapped package and pulled it out onto his lap.

"I've got some lemon candy. Would you like one?"

Her eyes brightened and she crawled toward him.

She'd just sat on her haunches and reached out her hand—the same one that had been in her mouth—for the piece of candy he offered when a voice rang out from beyond the canvas.

"Sarah?"

"In here," he returned.

The wagon jostled and there was Alice. The look of relief on her face hit him hard. She turned her head and shoulders to call out to someone behind her.

Another clap of thunder. In its wake, he realized the

growing sound of something hitting the canvas. Was the snow-fall growing more violent?

"Come inside," he said.

To his surprise, she did. Evangeline was on her heels, pushing Alice closer to him

She stepped gingerly away from his leg and glanced at the opening before perching on the edge of a crate.

"There isn't room," Alice protested.

"There's plenty," he said easily.

Evangeline glanced between them before she turned to tighten up the canvas, shrinking the opening.

Evangeline patted her hair as Alice hugged her snow-sprinkled shawl closer around her shoulders.

It was a tight squeeze, but such a relief to see anything other than the underside of that canvas roof. He started gathering up the papers so they'd have room to sit.

Lightning illuminated the entire inside of the wagon. Thunder followed, booming and shaking the entire wagon.

Sarah threw herself into her mother's lap.

Evangeline tugged her into a hug, whispering into her hair, "It's all right."

Another inspiration struck, and Rob reached for one of the blank pieces of paper from his stack. He began folding it, using his good leg as a sort of table.

"How did she get in here?" Evangeline asked, no hint of accusation in her voice.

He shrugged. "She opened the tie when the thunder started up."

Alice glanced at Evangeline. "I'm sorry she got away from me. We were hurrying back from the woods and her hand slipped from mine. By the time I blinked, she was gone in the snow."

"She must've thought this was our wagon," Evangeline said.

"She was in a hurry to get inside," he agreed.

Finished with his folding, he held out the creation—now resembling a frog flat on his palm. "See here," he told Sarah. And then he tapped the frog so it jumped from his palm onto the wagon bed.

The girl's face lit up. She squirmed off Evangeline's lap and made a beeline for the paper toy.

"Careful," Alice murmured, reaching out a hand to steady the girl and make sure she didn't bump Rob.

Sarah picked up the paper frog and waved it in Alice's direction.

"I see." She tipped her face the slightest bit in Rob's direction, giving him a hint of the smile she'd aimed at Sarah. "That's a fine trick."

"One of my tutors taught me. He'd learned it during a visit to Europe. I must've been about ten at the time. Grandfather wasn't amused at the line of frogs I left along the edge of his desk."

Evangeline smiled. "I wish one of my tutors would've taught me something so lighthearted. I think they were all frightened of my father."

Alice's smile had turned to a frown that she hid by ducking her head to play with Sarah, tapping the frog so it hopped along the wagon bed.

"My grandfather was difficult to please," he offered. "I frequently begged to be allowed to do my learning at the schoolhouse, but he was insistent that tutors would give a better education."

Evangeline nodded, her brows drawn as if she empathized, but it was Alice who asked, "Why did you want to go to school?"

He reached for another piece of paper and began folding idly as he spoke. "It was lonely in the big house. I prayed and prayed for a brother or sister, and once I learned that would never happen, I figured I could make friends at school."

Alice stared at Rob in confusion. "*You* were lonely?"

He tapped the frog back in Sarah's direction when it came close to him. "That surprises you?"

"I often prayed for a sister as well," Evangeline murmured.

"Yes, but—" Alice's stammer was adorable, and his lips started to lift into a smile. Until her eyes snapped at him.

He creased the final fold and then offered her the paper from his hand—a near-perfect heart.

Alice stared at it for long seconds before she shook her head and set her hands in her lap.

He lowered his own hand to his side. Caught the gaze Evangeline darted between the two of them.

"Leo hasn't told me how you two were connected back home."

Alice's expression tightened.

"I had the pleasure of meeting the fair Alice when she was helping my cousin Fannie try out the fit of a ball gown."

Alice's frown flattened. He wanted her to remember—

"I simply wanted to know her name, but she put me in my place."

Her eyes flashed at him before she gave a quick shake of her head. "I didn't—"

"And I was instantly smitten."

Color crept high into Alice's cheeks as she stared at him, eyes bright. "No—"

"Smitten," he repeated as he held her stare. "From that first moment. And I only came to admire Alice more deeply the more I came to know her."

* * *

"Hullo?"

Alice had never been so relieved to hear Leo's voice call out from beyond the wagon canvas. She was grateful for the chance to avert her face from Rob's intent stare.

"We're here!" Her own voice was shaky as she called out to him.

Evangeline tugged open the canvas cover, and Leo's head and shoulders filled the space, his glance quickly encompassing the small area. He didn't ask why his wife and adopted daughter were inside, which was a relief. Alice had been deathly frightened when Sarah had run off. She didn't want to relive it again, to tell her brother how she'd almost lost the girl.

Rob lifted a small paper parcel in offer. "Lemon candy?"

Leo's eyes glittered as he waved it off. "Storm's moving off. I'll get a fire started if you're of a mind to make supper."

Alice nodded, more than ready to escape from the confined space and the way Rob seemed to fill it completely with his presence.

Evangeline murmured for Sarah to "come along."

"I'm afraid I'm not up to cooking tonight," Rob drawled. "Maybe tomorrow."

Leo shot him a scathing glance that changed into something else. Leo motioned to the papers in a jumble at Rob's side. "What's all this?"

Rob's eyes narrowed slightly and for a moment it seemed as if he wouldn't answer, then, "Plans and sketches for my sawmill."

Evangeline paused, hand on Sarah's head.

Leo cleared his throat. "A sawmill?"

The way Rob's brows creased, it was obvious he was as confused by Leo's query as Alice was.

"When you said, 'mill,' I figured you meant to start up a powder mill, like the Old Man."

Alice winced at her brother's use of the nickname that almost everyone who worked in the Braddock mills and for the household called Rob's grandfather.

Rob seemed not to notice. "It would be too difficult to procure supplies to make gunpowder this far from civilization. Something like that won't be feasible for years yet. I've researched and made plans for a sawmill." He shot a glance in Alice's direction, a glance she couldn't return. "A mill to provide for me—and a family."

Leo's jaw locked tight.

Evangeline tipped her head. "My father sold his interest in the sawmills he'd helped found back in the East." She bit her lip. "He'd made plans much like yours. God rest his soul."

"Then I suppose we'll be competitors," Rob said slowly.

Alice hadn't made the connection until that very moment.

That's what had Leo riled up, and now what was causing Rob's deep frown.

"Will you carry on with his plans?" Rob asked.

Leo crossed his arms over his chest. "She doesn't have to decide what to do yet. The loss is still fresh."

Evangeline seemed to come to herself, looking down at Sarah as the girl began to try to climb on top of a barrel near the back of the wagon. "My father was the one with the knowledge to run a mill—not me."

"You've got plenty of knowledge," Leo said. "From all those books. You can run a sawmill if you've got a mind to." His chin jutted out stubbornly.

Evangeline smiled warmly at her husband. "I'm glad you think so. But maybe further discussion another time..." She caught Sarah as the little girl jumped off the barrel. "This one needs to get down and stretch her legs."

Evangeline handed Sarah to Leo and started to climb out of the wagon.

"Alice, stay—" Rob started.

But Alice couldn't. Not with his words, *smitten, admire,* whirling through her mind.

She didn't look at him as she clambered out of the wagon. "I'll bring your supper in a bit."

Leo squatted over a small pile of sticks and kindling, flint in hand.

He'd need more wood. On a cold night like tonight, the fire would burn through quickly. She moved to Leo's wagon, where Evangeline was bundling Sarah into a warm coat. Alice reached for some of the sticks and thin logs she and Evangeline had picked up during their walking time the past few days.

Evangeline trailed her to where Leo was building the fire. Alice deposited her armful of wood beside him. When he glanced up at her, she wasn't prepared for the sharp expression on his face.

"Why didn't you tell me?" he demanded quietly. "About you and Braddock? Back in New Jersey?"

Something sharp knotted inside her gut. Was this what Coop felt like on the other side of one of Leo's interrogations?

"There's nothing—"

"The man just admitted he's smitten with you," Evangeline countered. She only watched Alice for a moment before turning her head to keep an eye on Sarah, who was drawing patterns in the snow with her mittened hand.

Alice exhaled a frustrated sound. She wanted to hide. Avoid this conversation forever.

But she couldn't.

She hugged her shawl around her middle, felt heat prick the lobes of her ears.

"At first... it didn't feel real." Saying it aloud gave truth to what she'd kept inside for so long. "I thought his interest, the attention—would fade because of my station. We're so different..."

Evangeline laid a hand on Leo's shoulder as he fed more sticks into the flickering fire. "Sometimes differences can be a good thing. Iron sharpens iron."

The reminder of the Scripture from Ecclesiastes only tightened the knot inside Alice.

"I didn't tell you because... because I didn't want you to order me not to see him. Even at the risk of my job." Her breath caught. "I suppose there was a part of me that liked how being with him made me feel." She ducked her head for a moment to hide the tears that pricked her eyes. "When we spent time together, I felt as if I was the only thing important to him. It was... lovely to be the most important thing to someone else."

"You're important to me," Leo grumbled. "To Collin. And Coop."

Was she? Sometimes it didn't feel that way. Back in New Jersey, none of her brothers had even noticed when she'd spent time with Rob. During those weeks, Leo had brushed off her concerns about Coop. He'd been too busy, too wrapped up with his work, to pay attention.

"And then everything with the mill—with Coop—happened and—" She shook her head. Couldn't say the words aloud. She'd pleaded with Rob to find a way to keep Coop out of trouble after what had happened. And he'd refused.

She'd been mistaken about everything. Everything she'd believed about their relationship, about her importance to him.

"Even so, he followed you on this journey," Evangeline said quietly.

Leo looked pensive, as if this was the first time he'd had this realization.

Alice shook her head slowly. "I came to terms with it before we left home. There's no future for us."

Which was why it hurt so badly when Rob said things like he had in the wagon only minutes ago.

She bit her lip, but couldn't keep the words inside. "Do you think... do you think there's any chance Coop is innocent? That he didn't cause the explosion at the mill?"

He'd never outright claimed his innocence, although he'd

thrown out a claim that Leo refused to listen to during an argument she'd overheard months ago.

Leo's expression shuttered. He pushed up on his knees and straightened. "I don't know. He was drinking almost every night. Fighting." Her older brother ran his hands down his face. "I should've taken him off the line. Fired him. It would've been better than what happened."

She knew how deeply Leo had mourned the two men who'd died in that explosion. He'd felt a personal responsibility, though he hadn't been at work at the time. He'd once said he would never forgive himself.

Evangeline came close and laid a hand on his shoulder. He turned toward her and suddenly Alice was on the outside. She couldn't hear Evangeline's soft words. Sarah was at their feet, wiggling her way between their legs and into the embrace.

Alice was left to tend to supper. Take care of what needed done.

An emptiness gnawed inside her.

As she was passing Rob's wagon, a low groan from inside met her ears. She stopped at the side of the wagon. Spoke so he could hear her through the canvas. "Do you need anything?"

A pause, then, "Maybe some of that awful tea."

"I'll brew some."

If he was asking for the willow bark tea, which he'd clearly told her he hated, the pain must be bad. Should she fetch Doc, too?

She decided to bring the tea first and determine the severity of Rob's fever before she brought the doctor.

In a few minutes, she carefully climbed into the wagon,

holding the tea in a mug and balancing carefully so it wouldn't spill.

When she handed it to Rob, his fingers closed over hers for a moment too long. Long enough for goosebumps to prickle up her arm at the feel of his warm skin against hers.

He gazed at her over the rim of the cup. "The wind changed, I think. I couldn't hear all of it, but I heard you ask if Coop could be innocent."

It was the last thing she'd expected him to say, and she felt as if she'd taken a blow that knocked the wind out of her. Drat the thin canvas.

She dropped her gaze to the floor and tried to even her voice. "If you're going to tell me to stop being foolish, save your breath."

A moment's pause. "I was only going to say that your optimism is another thing I admire about you. Your belief that everyone can be good."

Her throat closed with emotion, and she left without another word.

Why couldn't he be cold and standoffish?

Leo and Evangeline were gone, and Alice desperately needed to start supper, but her eyes brimmed with sudden tears. She reached into her pocket for a handkerchief, and instead her fingers closed over folded paper.

She withdrew the small heart. Had Rob slipped it into her pocket as she'd leaned close to hand him the tea?

She cradled it in one hand, the other coming up to cover her lips as emotion rose inside her.

And then she registered the lines on the folded paper. She

unfolded it to reveal a pencil sketch. A log cabin, with light trees sketched in to reveal a forest beyond it.

A house. One that could be the home she'd been dreaming of for weeks on this journey. She traced the drawing with one finger, imagining curtains she might sew—not plain muslin, but something with a pattern. Wildflowers, maybe, or vines. In her mind, she could see herself in the doorway, flour on her apron from baking.

Was this what he imagined for them—what he'd wanted to give her before everything that had separated them?

The thought of it hurt too much, and her tears spilled free.

Seven

BELLE COULDN'T SHAKE the feeling of being watched.

It was late in the evening, but after a long day of travel, folks were still up and about.

A young, first-time mother laboring to have her baby had called away both Maddie and Jason at the same time. Before she left, Maddie had asked Belle to help the children finish their supper.

Belle couldn't say no, not when Maddie had done so much for her, with the sneaking and subterfuge to keep Belle hidden in the wagons for weeks before she'd been discovered.

The two boys were arguing over who got the last bite of biscuit from the pan while their little sister played on a quilt spread on the ground between the fire and the family's wagon. Belle tried to glance around the camp without being noticed.

"Tommy!" Alex called sharply. The little dog had his nose

to the ground, hackles raised as he stared toward the darkening tree line.

"What's got into him?" Paul wondered aloud.

Alex abandoned his plate to go to the little dog. The boy sent a worried look over his shoulder as he dragged Tommy back to their campsite and tied him off to the wagon with a short piece of rope. "You think there's something out there?"

A shiver shook Belle. Sarge. Sarge was out there somewhere.

Most folks were tidying up their campsites after supper, putting boxes and barrels in their wagons or pitching tents in the firelight. Some hurried through the dusk to the woods where a burbling creek could barely be heard.

There.

A man across camp, sitting on a barrel, whittling something. He wasn't paying any attention to the knife's rhythmic movements. He was staring at Belle.

Such a stare. She should be used to it by now, shouldn't she? Men looking at her with lust or disgust—she'd never figured it out. Were they disgusted with her, or with themselves? Somehow it seemed different out here, not being in the brothel and receiving the same stares she'd experienced there. This wasn't a tavern or back room of a saloon. This was a camp, with families and men chasing their fortunes.

Was that why this look bothered her more than when she'd been at Thaddeus's?

Or had she simply forgotten how to ignore a man's eyes in the weeks since she'd run away?

Belle kept her head down, fussing over Alex and Paul as they bickered, but her nerves vibrated like a plucked string. She knew what it meant when a man looked at a girl that way. It made her skin prickle beneath her threadbare shawl.

As she crouched next to the low campfire, she couldn't help noticing the threadbare hem of her skirt. But she had nothing else to wear, only the gown and shawl she'd had on the night she'd escaped.

Alex and Paul hunched over tin plates of beans and crumbled biscuit, shoveling food into their mouths as if the meal might disappear before they finished. Jenny made small hiccuping noises on the blanket beside the wagon wheel. But Belle never took her eyes fully off the shadows at the edge of the camp.

She reached for the battered tin cup and poured what was left of the watery coffee for the boys. "You finish your beans," she told them quietly.

The boys glanced up at her, both with wide eyes, then ducked their heads over their plates. Her eyes darted to Jenny, who was busy chewing on a crust of biscuit, curls falling into her face.

Belle's heart twisted. Jenny was too little to understand the dangers of this world. Belle tucked her shawl tighter across her chest and scanned the firelight's edge. The shadows pressed in, hiding anyone who might be watching.

A sudden laugh split the air as two women walked past the fire, arms linked. One of them—Belle thought her name was Mrs. Hastings—looked right at her, lips pinched as if she'd bitten into a sour fruit. The whisper that followed, meant for her friend but loud enough for Belle to catch, made her cheeks burn: "I don't see why a girl like that is allowed to stay on with the company. Hollis should kick her out. It's not right, not with the children about."

Belle ducked her head, a few strands of hair loose from her braid falling between her face and the world. It wasn't enough. She wished she could disappear.

The boys whispered to each other, oblivious to the hurtful comment, as Belle's mind raced. Maddie had promised to help Belle until the company reached Oregon. But Belle still hadn't come up with a plan for what she'd do then. She had no money. No skills to earn any—she would never go back to what she'd had to do to survive.

And Sarge was still out there somewhere. Still hunting Belle.

What was she going to do?

By now, the women had walked across camp. Belle's hands were still shaking when she heard another voice say her name. This one she recognized.

Alice. Coop's sister.

Something about the way Alice moved—always with purpose, never wasting so much as a gesture—eased Belle's nerves just a little. She set her jaw and focused on wiping biscuit crumbs from Jenny's mouth, not wanting to show how rattled she felt.

"Are they giving you trouble?" Alice sent a quick, warm look at the boys, who'd frozen mid-bicker to stare at her. "I hear there's a reward for any boy who helps clean up after supper."

Paul looked skeptical. "What kind of reward?"

"Maybe a story if you finish your chores before dark." Alice's tone was mild, but it left no room for argument.

"Alice tells the best stories," Alex said.

The boys scrambled to pick up their tin plates, tripping over each other in their eagerness.

Belle busied herself gathering the battered cups and stacking them in a neat pile. Was that all Alice wanted? To check on the boys?

"I brought these for you," Alice said quietly.

Belle glanced up. She hadn't realized until now that Alice held a bundle of cloth between her hands. A dress. Pale blue, the color of river ice, with a little sprig of dark blue embroidery at the collar and sleeves. A real dress, not like the threadbare dance-hall dress that was Belle's only possession. It wasn't new. Clearly, the seams had been taken in, then let out and stitched again, neat work done by hand. Beneath the folded cloth, the toes of two brown boots peeked out.

Belle stared at the bundle in Alice's hands. Felt her pulse ticking in her throat.

"I—can't pay you," she said, voice tight. She meant for it to come out polite, but the words sounded like a warning.

Alice's eyes were kind. "It's meant to be a gift."

Belle didn't reach for the things. She'd learned the hard way that gifts always came with a price. A dress, a ribbon, a meal. It didn't matter what shape the charity took; payment was always expected sooner or later.

Alice's lips formed a stubborn pinch. "Your dress won't last the weeks we've got left before we reach Oregon. And it's getting on toward winter. Those shoes weren't meant for regular work."

Belle's chin tipped up. She didn't dare look down at the

fancy shoes that blistered her feet. The leather soles were already coming apart from so much walking.

"I can't accept it." She tried to give the words some finality, even though saying them made her stomach twist into a knot. If she wore a regular dress, regular shoes, would men stop staring?

"Of course you can." Alice must've decided Belle wasn't going to reach for the dress and shoes, so she set them on the ground at Belle's feet. "You've helped Maddie and the children for days now. It's our turn to help you. Everyone needs a friend." This last was said without looking directly at Belle.

Belle's cheeks burned. She wanted to turn away, to shrink down until she was only smoke drifting off the fire. Pretty had been her friend. Most of the other girls had held themselves separate. Not Pretty. She'd warned Belle off of men who were unkind or violent. Kept a plate of supper warm when she could. Rocked Belle to sleep when she'd wept after an encounter that had left her with a scar on her hip.

For a moment, the memory of Pretty's laughter seemed to float on the wintry air. And then Belle's mind saw Pretty's lifeless hand flopped in the dirt, sticky with blood.

Belle stared at the dress and the boots, aware of Alice standing patiently at her side. "You don't want to be friends with me."

I can't be friends with you.

If she truly believed that Alice wanted nothing more than friendship—which she wasn't certain she could believe—and befriended the woman, it would put Alice in Sarge's crosshairs. He'd killed Pretty without a second thought. Taken shots at both Coop and Rob, nearly killed them. He was merciless.

It would be safer for Alice to stay far, far away from Belle.

But a tiny part inside her wished things could be different.

So when Alice said, "I'd like to try," Belle swallowed the argument that wanted to be expressed. And reached for the fine dress.

* * *

Legs outstretched, Rob sat close to one of the campfires after the evening meal had been cleared away and most folks had settled in for the night. The flames cast dancing shadows across the collection of materials spread on the ground beside him—longer pieces of sturdy saplings he'd swallowed his pride and asked Leo to cut for him, thin strips of leather cord for lashing, and his pocket knife.

Ignoring the ache that still made him want to grit his back teeth, he picked up one of the smaller pieces of wood and resumed his whittling, shaving off thin curls that fell to the dirt beside him. His splinted leg made everything awkward. That's why he needed something to keep his hands busy.

The crutch was taking shape slowly. He'd measured it against his height as best he could while sitting, and now he worked on smoothing the crosspiece that would fit under his arm. Maybe Alice had some spare fabric he could use for padding—though asking her for anything seemed to set her on edge these days.

Movement across the camp caught his attention. Collin was carrying Stella into the circle of firelight, his arms strong around his wife's fragile frame. She must have needed to tend to private business in the woods. Even from this distance, Rob could see the tight lines of pain around her mouth, the way she held herself rigid against any jarring movement.

Stella said something to her husband that Rob couldn't make out over the crackle of the fire, but he saw her motion toward the flames and then toward him. Collin's expression darkened with what looked like reluctance, but then he moved in Rob's direction and finally he settled her gently on the wooden crate that Leo had used during supper before moving off to their wagon.

"You must be tired of being stuck in the wagon all day," Rob said, setting down his knife and giving Stella his attention.

Despite the pallor of her face and the way she pressed one hand to her side, she managed a wan smile. "I am. I'm ready to be up and about."

Collin returned from their wagon with a quilt draped over his arm, and Rob caught the frown that creased the man's features as he knelt to spread the blanket on the ground. When he straightened, his voice was gentle but firm.

"You need to rest, like Doc said. You need to heal."

The weight behind his words made Rob think of things left unsaid. The baby. No one had told him if Stella had lost the child when she'd been shot, but the careful way everyone treated her, the unspoken worry in Collin's eyes, told its own story.

"What are you working on?" Collin asked, nodding toward the wood pieces at Rob's side.

Rob held up the partially finished project. "I'm making a crutch."

Stella's eyes lit with something that might have been vindication. "See? He's tired of sitting around all day too."

Rob met her gaze and saw the frustration there that matched his own restlessness. "I've got plans that I need to get a start on, now that we're only a few weeks away from reaching the Willamette Valley."

He'd spent weeks preparing for this venture, but now the reality of starting over in a new place, of building something from nothing, felt both thrilling and daunting. Especially with his leg.

"What are your plans once you reach the valley?" Rob asked.

Collin's answer came immediately. "Rest. She's going to rest until the doctor says otherwise."

Stella pulled a face at her husband's protectiveness and huffed out a breath that held more than a little impatience. "Maybe it would help if I knew how to sew or knit. At least I could have something to do with my hands."

Rob considered this for a moment, then picked up his pocket knife and selected a small piece of wood from his pile. He held both out to her.

Collin's expression tightened with obvious disapproval, but Stella took the knife and wood eagerly, turning the chunk over in her hands thoughtfully.

"I'm a little worried the skills I learned after all those years in the factory aren't fit for making a home for our family." She wasn't really talking to Rob. Collin tipped his head forward so his forehead rested on her shoulder.

Rob wouldn't say so, but he understood. Since he'd been a boy, he'd planned—been prepared in every way—to one day take over the Braddock Powder Mills. Making the decision to leave, to go his own way had been one of the most difficult things he'd ever done. But it would all be worth it. He couldn't lose hope now.

Collin ran one finger along Stella's forearm in a tender gesture not meant for Rob's eyes. "You were providing for your sisters. It doesn't matter whether you can sew or cook. We'll make do."

The devotion in Collin's voice made something twist in Rob's chest. He wanted the kind of relationship Collin had with his wife for himself and Alice. He cleared his throat.

"I could use someone like you working at my mill," Rob said to Collin. "You were a hard worker for Grandfather's mill. You could even be a foreman."

Despite everything that had happened with Coop, Rob had always respected Collin's steady competence, his attention to detail. The man had a good head on his shoulders and knew how to keep his men in line.

Stella looked over at her husband with obvious pride, but Collin's expression was carefully blank. "I don't know what the future holds yet."

Was he holding back because of the trouble Coop caused back home? Rob was offering him a good opportunity.

Alice bustled into camp at that moment, her arms wrapped around what looked like a bundled quilt. She moved with that determined efficiency he'd come to recognize. The firelight caught the auburn highlights in her hair, and Rob felt that familiar tug in his chest.

"I'm determined to be a part of this family," Rob said, keeping his voice low so she wouldn't hear. "Alice would like it if we could work together."

Stella's brows went up even as Collin's eyes narrowed.

Collin shook his head, not unkindly. The man clearly didn't want to argue, and Rob could appreciate that. Collin had always been a peacemaker—Rob had seen it plenty of times at the mill when tensions ran high or tempers flared. It was something to value in a potential partner.

But more than that, Rob realized, it was something he needed to learn for himself. If he was going to win Alice's trust back, if he was going to earn his place in this family that meant everything to her, he'd have to stop pushing so hard and learn the art of patience.

Eight

ALICE RIFLED through the crates and other items scattered in the back of Rob's wagon, pushing aside bundles wrapped in oilcloth and wooden boxes that rattled with their contents. The canvas overhead filtered the late afternoon light, casting everything in a golden hue that made it difficult to distinguish one item from another.

A noise startled her—the scrape of a boot against the wagon's tailgate. She whirled around to find Coop peering in through the canvas covering.

"What are you doing?" he asked.

Her heart was still hammering from the surprise, but she also felt a beat of warmth that he'd sought her out. "I'm looking for a specific parcel that Rob asked me to find." She glanced around at all the things inside the wagon. "It's about this big" —she held her hands a foot apart—"and it's supposed to be somewhere in here." It felt as if she was looking for a needle in a haystack.

"Do you want some help?"

Another beat of surprise and she had to bite her lip to hide her smile when she nodded. It'd been days since they'd spoken. He'd skulked around the edges of camp, riding with the cattle all day and eating with the hired cowboys in the evening.

The wagon creaked and tipped slightly as he stepped up into it. They bumped elbows before she moved to the far end, weaving between the carefully packed belongings. She rolled up Rob's pallet so she and Coop didn't track dirt all over the place where he slept.

Coop bent to poke behind a crate in one corner. "Can't believe he packed all this stuff. Enough food to feed an entire family." He nudged one of two kegs of gunpowder with the toe of his boot. He picked up something from a nearby crate—an ornate silver tea service that would have been more suitable for a lady's parlor than their current surroundings. He turned the delicate sugar bowl in his hands, eyebrows raised. "This must've cost more than most folks see in a year. What's he gonna do with it out here?"

Alice didn't know if she should agree with him—or remind him that Rob could set up his future household any way he wanted. For a moment, when the sugar bowl caught a gleam of sunlight, her stomach twisted. Rob claimed he'd thought about marriage. To her. Somehow, it hurt.

Coop set the tea service aside and continued rummaging. When he spoke again, it was in an offhand tone. "I saw you with Belle earlier. What did you say to her?"

Alice glanced up from where she squatted. Coop was pretending to be casual about the subject. But she'd known him his whole life and saw through him.

"I noticed in the woods the other day that her gown wasn't surviving the trail very well so I gave her one of my old dresses."

She didn't tell him about the flash of vulnerability that had crossed the other woman's expression, gone so quickly it almost wasn't there. It had stirred Alice's compassion.

"I'm surprised you'd want anything to do with Belle," he said, still looking away.

Alice kept her attention on the wooden chest she'd propped open. "It seems Belle is important to you," she said quietly, "which means she's important to me too." She couldn't help continuing. "I think that someone with her... background likely has wounds that you and I can't imagine."

The words hung in the air. When she glanced up, Coop was staring at her with a hooded expression.

"There are some wounds that only God can heal, Coop."

He ducked his head, but not before she saw the way his jaw tightened stubbornly.

Then his expression shifted to curiosity. He toed one of the wagon's floorboards. Or rather, a wide crack between two boards.

He squatted and tapped on the board. "Hollow," he determined. He ran his fingers along the crack. "Probably a false bottom."

"Coop, leave it." Whatever was hidden under there was Rob's business, not theirs. "We shouldn't—"

But Coop was already working his fingers under the edge of the boards.

He waggled his eyebrows at her with the first genuine smile

she'd seen from him in days. "I wonder what he's got hidden in here. Probably a bunch of gold coins."

When he pulled up the hidden compartment, they both stared down at the contents. No gold coins. Instead, the space was filled with something large and flat, carefully wrapped in canvas and resting on a bed of sawdust. Of course Coop reached for the canvas. When he pulled it back, Alice recognized the large saw blade and an assortment of metal tools.

Coop looked flummoxed, but Alice knew this was Rob's investment in his future. It had to represent hundreds of dollars worth of equipment, packed away with such care that each piece was cushioned and secured. These were the tools he'd need for the sawmill he'd told Leo about.

"Let's close it up," she said quietly.

As Coop began replacing the floorboards, she finally spotted the brown twine-wrapped package she'd been looking for tucked into one corner of the wagon.

Alice retrieved it and then bent to spread out the pallet that Rob had been sleeping on, smoothing the rough blankets with careful hands. The familiarity of the task—tending to someone's comfort—stirred up a restless feeling in her chest.

"He seems much improved," Coop said, his voice deliberately casual. "Maybe you don't need to keep waiting on him hand and foot. You're not a servant in his household anymore."

Alice went quiet, her hands stilling on the blanket. The words cut deeper than they should have.

"Rob got hurt saving your life," she said finally.

Coop moved to the back of the wagon and started clambering out. His nose wrinkled as he reached for her to hand her down. "That's why you're taking care of him? As some kind of penance?"

When she didn't answer immediately, he continued, his voice growing heated. "That man out in the woods was trying to kill us both, Alice. Rob didn't save me—he was trying to save his own hide too."

Maybe he was right, but it didn't change the fact that Rob needed help.

"It's the right thing to do," Alice said.

Coop shook his head in disgust. "He's got to you, hasn't he? You dreamin' of being the one using that tea set?"

Hurt and frustration seethed inside her. "You know that won't happen."

"Rob and I will never get along." His voice dropped to barely above a whisper. "So if you choose him, you'll never see me."

The words hit her like a physical blow. Before she could form a response, Coop stalked away from the wagon.

Alice took a moment to steady her breath before she rounded the wagon, package in hand. Rob remained by the fire, tying a leather strap around two pieces of wood. Collin must've taken Stella to their tent, because Rob was alone now.

She held out the package to him. "Is this what you were looking for?"

Instead of taking it, Rob gently pushed it back toward her. There was something too intense in his eyes for her to meet his gaze directly.

"It's for you. A gift."

A gift?

She was aware of Coop across the campsite, squatting by the fire, pouring himself a cup of coffee. He was close enough to see them clearly, though probably too far away to overhear their conversation.

"Open it," Rob urged.

With trembling fingers, Alice unwrapped the brown paper. The fabric that spilled out took her breath away—a dress more beautiful than anything she'd ever owned. A deep blue silk that would bring out her eyes, with delicate lace at the collar and cuffs. Definitely not suitable for life on the trail. It would be fancier than her finest Sunday dress, though not quite at the level that his cousin Miss Pence would have worn. But it was beautiful, expensively made, and clearly chosen with care.

Heat flooded her cheeks as she stared down at the gorgeous fabric. Part of her wanted to hold it up to herself, to imagine how it might feel to wear something so fine. But the rational part of her mind was already folding it back up.

"I can't take it," she said, her voice barely steady. "It's too fine. And I don't need any kind of reward for taking care of you."

Rob gently pushed it back toward her, and when she glanced up, the expression in his eyes made her breath catch. "Alice, I bought it for you."

She sent a sideways glance across the campsite. Coop was watching them closely now. Everything he'd just said in the wagon rang in her ears. *He's got to you, hasn't he?*

Everything with Rob was too confusing. He pushed too hard, expected too much. Her hands shook as she folded the dress back into its paper wrapping.

"I can't take it," she said, standing abruptly and turning away before she could see the hurt surely written across his face.

* * *

Rob saw the look Alice darted toward her brother across the campsite. This was about more than what lay between him and Alice. Coop was involved somehow, and that realization frustrated him enough to push up off the ground.

"Come on," he muttered, more to himself than to her.

He felt his face flush as he used the crate and his handmade crutch to struggle to his feet. The wood bit into his armpit and every movement sent jolts of fire through his healing leg. But he couldn't just let her walk away.

He hobbled after Alice, awkward and painful as it was, his crutch sinking slightly into the soft earth with each step. She must have heard him because she whirled around to face him, her eyes wide with alarm.

"You shouldn't be up."

But he pushed forward, the words spilling out before he could stop them. "Whatever Coop said to you has nothing to do with us. He's doing his best to wreck your family. Don't let him come between us."

Alice's chin lifted stubbornly. "That's not what I'm doing."

But even as she argued with him, uncertainty flickered in her eyes, her gaze returning over and over to the place where Coop had walked off into the darkness. The frustration that had been building in Rob for days—watching her pull away— finally boiled over.

He closed the distance between them in two awkward steps and silenced her with a kiss.

It started as a storm—desperate, frustrated, all the emotion he'd been holding back crashing through him like thunder. His free hand came up to cup her face, his fingers trembling against her cheek as he poured everything he couldn't say into the pressure of his lips against hers.

But then something shifted. The fierce urgency gentled, became something tender and pleading. His thumb traced the line of her cheekbone as his mouth moved softly over hers, asking rather than demanding.

And Alice responded. She leaned into him, her hand coming up to rest against his chest. For a moment that felt like eternity, she kissed him back, her lips warm and yielding beneath his.

Then she was pulling away, her breathing unsteady as she pressed her fingertips to her lips. He kept his hold on her arms, feeling unsteady himself.

"That was a mistake," she whispered.

"No." His voice came out rougher than he'd intended. "It wasn't."

"Let me go."

"I can't." He tipped his head and followed her gaze to where his crutch had fallen on the ground. Right now he was balancing on one foot.

"I'm afraid if I move wrong, I'll fall," he muttered.

Her eyes connected with his. Maybe it was the vulnerability he'd shared, but her expression softened with understanding before she dipped her face so he couldn't read her.

It was awkward for a minute as she bent to retrieve his

crutch, her movements careful as she helped steady him against her shoulder.

"You overdid it, didn't you?" The knowing look in her eyes made his chest tighten.

She came around to settle under his arm, her own arm circling his waist to help support his weight as they slowly made their way back toward his wagon.

"I'm not sorry for the kiss," he said quietly. "But I am sorry for how it started."

Alice was silent for a long moment, her steps carefully matched to his halting pace. Finally, she said, "Why do you do that?"

"What?"

"Push so hard when you lose your temper. When you lose control of yourself."

Heat climbed up Rob's neck. "It doesn't end well," he admitted.

They reached his wagon, and Alice paused, clearly waiting for him to explain. He rubbed the back of his neck with his free hand, feeling exposed in a way that made his skin crawl. He didn't love her seeing this vulnerability, this weakness in him.

"I never should have let myself lose control," he said.

"What do you mean?"

Rob stared at the wagon canvas for a moment, old anger stirring in his chest. The familiar scent of wood smoke brought back memories he'd tried to bury.

"When I was fifteen, Grandfather started me working at the powder mill." He shifted his weight, grateful for Alice's steady support. "Not in the office or keeping books like you might expect. He put me to work doing the most menial jobs he could find."

Alice remained silent, but he felt her attention like a physical thing.

"I spent my days hauling wheelbarrows full of saltpeter and sulfur until my shoulders ached." The old frustration heated his voice. "Fetching firewood in all kinds of weather. Stoking the fires that kept the grinding mills running." He paused. "I thought it was temporary. That once I'd proven myself, Grandfather would move me to something more... suitable."

"But he didn't?" Alice asked quietly.

"No." Rob's jaw tightened. "There was this fellow, Thomas Henley. Maybe nineteen, been working there since he was younger than I was. He made it his mission to provoke me."

He could still picture Thomas clearly—stocky build, perpetual sneer, hands permanently stained with gunpowder residue. "He'd wait until the foreman was out of earshot, then start needling. 'Look at the little lord getting his hands dirty.' Day after day, pushing to see how far he could go."

Alice made a soft sound, and Rob found himself continuing.

"I tried to keep my head down. Grandfather had made it clear that complaining wasn't an option." Rob's free hand clenched. "But Thomas kept escalating. And then one day, he said something about my mother. Something cruel about her dying young."

The memory flashed hot and sharp. "I threw a punch. Connected with his jaw—felt good for about three seconds." His voice went flat. "Then he beat me bloody in front of half the workers."

Rob shook his head, the old fury still simmering beneath his ribs. "But here's the thing—Thomas wanted me to hit him. He'd been baiting me for weeks, and I finally gave him exactly what he was looking for. An excuse."

"What happened after?"

"Grandfather fired Thomas. But then sat me down and said the whole thing was my fault for losing my temper. That if I'd kept control, nothing would have happened." Rob's voice went hard. "He blamed me for being manipulated instead of being angry at Thomas for the manipulation."

He felt Alice's hand tighten on his arm.

"That's when I learned the real lesson—it wasn't about fighting back. It was about not letting people like Thomas control when and how I fight. Losing my temper gave him all the power." Rob paused. "And I've spent years trying not to make that mistake again."

"I walked around in pain for weeks afterward," he continued. "Had a bruised rib that made it agony to lift anything heavier than a book. Every breath felt like someone was driving a knife between my ribs. But Grandfather didn't take it easy on me. If anything, he worked me harder."

"Actions have consequences," she said simply.

He watched as her gaze drifted toward the far edge of camp, where the cowboys were bedding down with the cattle for the night. Where Coop would be.

"Everyone loses control sometimes, Rob," she said softly. "The Bible says we all sin and fall short of God's glory. It doesn't make you a bad person. It only makes you human."

Something hot and tight lodged in his throat at her words. Without thinking, he reached out to touch her cheek, his thumb grazing the soft skin there. But she jerked away from him, the moment of understanding broken.

"Good night, Rob," she said awkwardly.

"Good night, Alice."

He watched her walk away, knowing that something had changed between them tonight—but uncertain if it was for better or worse.

Nine

"FASTER!" Ben shrieked as she and Alex each grabbed one of Alice's hands and spun her around in a dizzying circle.

"C'mon! Faster!" Alex's voice cracked with laughter as they whirled between the other dancers—men and women stepping lively to Collin's fiddle music while children wove in and out among them like excited puppies.

Alice's skirts billowed out as the kids increased their pace, pulling Alice so fast that her feet barely touched the ground. Around them, couples laughed and clapped to the rhythm, their faces bright with firelight from the several blazes lit in the center of the circled wagons.

"I'm getting dizzy!" Alice gasped, but she was laughing too, caught up in the children's infectious joy.

The company was celebrating. Three weeks—that's all that remained of their long journey to the Willamette Valley. The thought should have filled Alice with joy, but even as she spun with the children, all she could think about was the kiss.

Two days had passed since Rob had pulled her into his arms, since his lips had claimed hers with that desperate intensity that had gentled into something achingly tender. Two days, and she still couldn't stop the memory from flooding through her at the most inconvenient moments. The way his thumb had traced her cheek. The way she'd leaned into him, her traitorous heart responding before she'd come to her senses.

She'd tried to put distance between them since then. Kept busy with endless tasks, avoided lingering near the campfire, asked Leo to intervene when Rob needed help. But every time she caught his eye across the camp, he leveled a look on her—as if he could see straight through her to the longing she was trying so hard to deny.

Alice spun little Ben around in a circle, the girl's delighted laughter mixing with the lively music that Collin coaxed from his instrument. Alex darted between the dancers, nearly colliding with couples as he chased after a barking Tommy.

Even now Alice was aware of Rob watching her. When their gazes clashed through the dancing pioneers, his eyes were warm with that familiar intensity that made her stomach flutter. The memory of his kiss crashed over her again. She had to look away, heat flooding her cheeks.

"Catch me, Miss Alice!" Ben called out as she broke away from her and raced toward the edge of the firelight.

Alice gave chase, her skirts swishing around her legs, until she was breathless and had to step aside from the dancing. Her chest rose and fell rapidly as she pressed a hand to her side, trying to catch her breath. She kept watching Ben as the girl danced around on her own.

"Alice, would you hold Molly for a bit?" Owen appeared at

her elbow, his baby daughter fussing in his arms. "I'd like to ask my wife to dance."

Alice looked past him to where Rachel was laughing at something Evangeline said, the two women standing near a wagon.

"She's been a little fussy today," Owen said, "I'll come get her if need be."

"That's all right, Owen. Go ahead and dance with Rachel." Alice reached for the baby, settling the small bundle against her shoulder.

Owen's face lit with gratitude before he hurried over to claim his wife for the next song.

Molly began crying almost immediately. Not wanting Rachel to miss her dance, Alice rocked her gently, bouncing slightly as she made her way around the edges of the celebration.

The baby's cries grew louder despite Alice's efforts to calm her. She found herself moving toward the edge of the firelight, where Rob sat on a stack of two wooden crates. He'd been up and around more on his crutch over the past few days, though she could tell he was still in considerable pain. Doc seemed watchful, worried the infection would come back.

Molly's wails intensified, and Alice patted her back feeling increasingly flustered. Nothing she tried seemed to comfort the baby.

From his perch on the crates, Rob motioned for Alice to come closer. What now?

He held out his arms. Alice's throat tightened with something she couldn't name, but she reluctantly handed over the baby, ready to take Molly back the moment Rob desired.

But to her surprise, Rob settled the baby on his shoulder, one large hand supporting the baby's back, and whispered something too soft for Alice to hear. Within moments, the baby's cries subsided to hiccups, then to silence. She snuggled into his shoulder.

Something inside Alice warmed and twisted at the sight. The tenderness in Rob's expression as he looked down at the sleeping child, the careful way he held her. It painted a picture of the father he might someday be.

"I was wondering whether you were going to come over here or keep avoiding me," he said quietly, his voice carrying just enough teasing to make her defensive.

"I'm not avoiding you," she protested, not quite truthfully.

He leveled that knowing look on her, the one that said he could see through her pretenses.

She forced a laugh and gestured toward the dancing couples. "I'm surprised you aren't up and dancing."

Rob's expression shifted to teasing. "My leg's not quite ready for that."

She needed to change the subject. "How did you get her to calm down?"

Rob's smile made her stomach dip dangerously. "It's a secret."

Alice caught sight of Owen and Rachel across the clearing. When she nodded and tipped her head toward Rob to indicate that he had successfully calmed the baby, Owen's relieved smile was visible even from this distance. The couple continued dancing, Rachel's hand in her husband's.

"What are you going to do when all your brothers have settled down?" Rob asked, his gaze on the dancers.

The question caught her off guard. "What do you mean?"

"Aren't you going to want a family of your own?"

The words sent a jolt through her, too close to dreams she'd tried to bury. Images flashed through her mind—a home of her own, children with dark hair and Rob's warm eyes—a life that seemed as distant as the stars overhead.

Alice's gaze drifted across the camp, landing on August where he sat with Felicity near one of the other fires. Even from here, she could see the tension between them, the careful distance Felicity maintained.

Needing another distraction, she said, "August told me you offered him a job at your mill."

"That's right."

August had sounded so surprised when he'd told her about Rob's offer. Surprised, but then there had been a hint of life in his voice, a spark of interest that had been missing since he'd lost his sight. Rob had done that for him, given her half-brother something to hope for again.

"This would have been the perfect night to wear your new dress," Rob said, his voice taking on a teasing note. The dress. Why had Rob done it? A way to win her? She couldn't quite ask. Rob's gaze was distant on the dancers.

Alice shook her head firmly. "That dress belongs to you."

"Everything I have is yours."

The simple words hit her hard, stealing the breath from her lungs. The absolute conviction in his voice, the way he looked at her as if she were the most precious thing in his world—it was too much.

"Rob..." she whispered, but couldn't find words to finish the thought.

Around them, the music swelled and dancers laughed, but Alice felt as if she were suspended in a bubble of silence, caught in the gravitational pull of Rob's unwavering gaze and the promise that hung unspoken between them.

* * *

Rob felt the weight of baby Molly settle more heavily against his shoulder as her breathing began to even out. She was drifting off despite the noise of the music and crowd. He shifted slightly to better support her, careful of his leg.

Alice's gaze had eased away from him, and he followed her line of sight to where Coop stood in the shadows between two wagons. Alice's younger brother leaned against the wagon's side, arms crossed, his posture radiating the kind of stubborn isolation Rob recognized all too well. Coop wasn't participating in the celebration—that much was clear. And his attention was focused intently on Doc and Maddie's wagon, watchful in a way that made Rob suspect Belle was hidden inside.

"Someday, he's gonna appreciate how you've watched over him," Rob said quietly.

Alice swallowed hard, her throat working as if the words were difficult to get out. "I wish my mama was still alive. She would know what to do with him, how to draw him back into the family."

As she spoke, Alice shifted slightly closer to where he sat, close enough that he could catch the faint scent of soap in her hair. Rob seized the moment, reaching over with his free hand to clasp her fingers in his. Her hand was smaller than his, work-roughened but warm, and she didn't pull away immediately.

Molly gave a soft burp against his shoulder and then settled completely, her breathing deepening into the rhythm of sleep. Holding the baby stirred something tender and protective in his chest.

"I've prayed and prayed that God would move in his life and bring him back to us," Alice said, her voice thick with emotion. "And then... I don't know. I should have known that it wouldn't matter or it wouldn't do any good."

She gently disengaged her hand from his, and Rob felt the loss of that connection like a physical ache. There was something in her voice, a resignation that went deeper than just worry for Coop.

"What do you mean?" Rob asked gently.

Alice shifted, not meeting his eyes. "It's nothing. I shouldn't have said—"

"Alice." His voice was quiet but firm. "What do you mean?"

For a moment, he thought she might refuse to answer. Her gaze fixed on the dancers swirling around the fires, on the shadows between the wagons, on the darkness beyond. Anywhere but on him. But then her shoulders sagged slightly, as if the weight of whatever she was carrying had become too much to bear alone.

"When I was fourteen, my ma got really sick. Really fast." The words came out in a rush, as if she needed to get them out before she lost her courage. Her fingers plucked at her skirt, a nervous gesture that made Rob's chest tighten. "One night, I sat up with her and prayed over her for hours. I prayed that God wouldn't take her. I needed my mama still."

Around them, the dancing continued in full swing—Collin's fiddle sang out a lively tune, couples laughed as they spun around the fires, children shrieked with delight as they chased each other. But here, in this small space beside his makeshift seat, it felt as if they were surrounded by a bubble of quiet grief that the noise couldn't penetrate.

She pressed her lips together as if trying to hold back words—or tears. Her breathing had grown shallow.

She didn't say the rest, but Rob could fill in the terrible conclusion. Her mother had died anyway, leaving Alice and her brothers to fend for themselves.

The familiar ache of loss settled in his own chest. He knew that desperate, bargaining kind of prayer all too well—the kind where you promised God anything if He would just let the person you loved most stay with you. He'd been even younger when his mother and father had perished in an accident, but he remembered sleepless nights praying that Mr. Phillip's letter was wrong, that they would come back.

"How old were your brothers?" he asked gently, his voice rough with remembered grief.

"Leo was fifteen. The twins were twelve."

Rob's heart clenched at the picture she painted—children trying to hold together the fragments of their shattered family, with Alice barely more than a child herself suddenly thrust into the role of mother and caretaker.

"There's a lot of people in need, and I know that God doesn't always answer our prayers the way we want Him to," Alice continued, her voice barely above a whisper. "But in those desperate moments, I needed the answer to be yes, and He didn't hear me."

Rob let his hand close around hers again, his fingers gentle but insistent as he tugged her slightly toward him, wanting her to look at him. He hated feeling so helpless, wished he had the strength to stand up and draw her into his arms properly. Her eyes were brimming with unshed tears, and the firelight flickered across her hair, turning the auburn strands to gold.

His voice sounded rougher than he'd intended. "God heard your prayer. He just—"

"How could He?" Alice interrupted, her eyes flashing with a pain that went soul-deep. "If He heard me, if He really cared, then why did He let her die? Why did He leave us alone?"

She pulled her hand away to wipe at a tear that had escaped to track down her cheek, and Rob felt the distance between them like a chasm he didn't know how to cross.

"I don't know why she had to die, but the Good Book says He knew you when you were still in your mother's womb."

Her eyes focused on the far off distance. Coop had gone now. Owen and Rachel appeared to claim the sleeping baby. Alice disappeared before Rob could stop her.

He wanted to talk more. Wanted to know her hurts, her fears. Was she ever going to let him in?

Ten

SOFT SNOWFLAKES DRIFTED DOWN from the gray morning sky, dusting the ground with a fine layer of white that crunched softly underfoot. The wagon train was minutes away from the bugle signaling departure, and Alice heard the familiar sounds of breaking camp—the jingle of harnesses, the creak of wagon wheels, the low voices of travelers making final preparations.

Alice finished securing the last of her belongings in the wagon when movement caught her eye. Rob was returning from the woods, moving slowly and carefully with the aid of his crutch. Each step seemed deliberate, measured, and she found herself watching the determined set of his shoulders as he navigated the uneven ground.

God heard your prayer. He knew you before you were born.

His words from the night before echoed in her mind, stirring up that same confusing tangle of emotions she'd been trying to sort through since their conversation by the fire. The way he'd looked at her when she'd told him about her mother, the gentleness in his voice. His response had cracked something open inside her that she'd kept carefully sealed. Until now.

She needed to decide. Either shut him out completely and go back to the careful distance she'd been trying to maintain. Or...

She couldn't quite finish the thought.

A shout, sharp and angry, cut through the morning air. Alice whipped her head around, searching for the source. Most of the other wagons had already moved out, but she spotted Belle huddled at the back of Doc and Maddie's wagon, wearing the dress Alice had given her. Two men were crowding her, their postures aggressive, predatory. One looked to be in his thirties, tall and lanky with greasy hair beneath a worn hat. The other was younger, maybe mid-twenties, stockier, with a patchy beard that made him look unkempt.

"Come now, miss," the older one was saying, his voice carrying a false sweetness that made Alice's skin crawl. "No need to be shy. We got coin to spend."

Alice started toward the wagon. "Pretty dress," the younger man added with a leer, stepping closer despite Belle's obvious distress. "Bet you look even prettier without it."

Belle pressed herself harder against the wagon, a knife trembling in her white-knuckled grip.

The shout had come from Coop, who was rushing forward to intervene.

"Get away from her!" Coop's voice carried clearly now.

But the men didn't back down as he joined the group. Alice was still yards away. The older one turned toward Coop with a smirk.

"Well, well. Look who's come to play protector," he drawled.

"Mind your own business, boy," the stockier man added. "We saw her first."

If anything, they seemed emboldened by Coop's approach, as if his youth made him less of a threat.

"Alice, stop!" Rob's voice called out behind her, registering over her heartbeat hammering in her ears.

She couldn't stop. She could only focus on the scene unfolding ahead. Coop tried to shoulder in between Belle and the two men, but they weren't deterred. One stepped to the side, trying to block him.

By the time Alice reached them, Belle was backed against the wagon, the knife trembling in her hand, her face pale with terror. She seemed lost in her own thoughts, her eyes wide and unseeing.

"Belle, get in the wagon," Alice said firmly, touching the girl's arm.

Belle jumped at the contact, the knife jerking in her grip.

Only feet away, the three men formed a tense triangle, voices rising in argument. Alice tried to catch Coop's attention.

"Coop, leave it alone," she said, but he ignored her.

"Go away," Coop told the men, his voice low and danger-ous. "She doesn't want you around."

Beard sneered. "She didn't say that."

Coop's fury spiked so fast Alice could almost feel the heat of it. "She doesn't have to say it. You're gonna leave her alone!"

One of the men spat at Coop's feet. The other shoved him hard in the chest.

Everything erupted into chaos. Coop's fist connected with

the older man's jaw. The stockier man lunged forward. Bodies collided. Grunts and curses filled the air. The older man swung wild. Missed. Stumbled backward. Coop ducked. Came up swinging, and connected. Alice heard the sound of flesh meeting flesh. The younger man grabbed Coop's shirt. Yanked hard. Fabric tore. Alice heard Rob shouting something from behind her, but the words were lost in the melee.

Without thinking, she reached for her brother's arm, trying to pull him back from the violence.

An elbow caught her in the jaw, sending stars exploding across her vision. Before she could recover, a fist connected with her midsection, driving the air from her lungs and throwing her to the ground.

A gunshot cracked through the morning air.

Everyone froze.

Rob, still moving slowly on his crutch, held a rifle pointed skyward, smoke rising from the barrel. His face was set in hard lines Alice had never seen before.

The commotion had drawn Leo, who came riding in, frustration etched deeply on his face. Alice's jaw throbbed with pain as she struggled to her feet, tasting blood where she'd bitten her lip.

Coop's nose dripped blood, his hat was gone, dark hair disheveled and his shirt torn askew. The other two men were equally rumpled, one sporting a fresh scrape across his cheek. All three looked ready to resume fighting at the slightest provocation.

Leo slid off his horse. "Get your wagons ready or I'll report you to Hollis," he ordered the two men, his voice carrying the authority of command.

They glared but moved away, muttering under their breaths.

Leo rounded on Coop next. "I told you to leave that girl alone!"

"And I told you I aim to protect her," Coop shot back, wiping blood from his nose with the back of his hand.

"You're gonna get yourself thrown out of the company for fighting."

Coop's eyes glittered with defiance as Alice reached for his arm.

She expected some concern, but Coop shook her off and stomped away. Leo turned on her, his face set in furious lines.

"I told you to stay away from him! He's making bad choices, and he's not acting like a Spencer."

"Leo, he's—"

"I don't want to hear it, Alice." His dismissive tone cut like a blade. "Stay out of Coop's way or you'll keep getting hurt."

He walked away, leaving her standing there with her jaw aching and her heart breaking. So he had noticed? She touched her lip, her fingers coming away with blood on them, and breathed through her tears.

Alice found Coop leaning against the side of the wagon that Belle had disappeared inside of, his jaw clenched tight, a muscle jumping beneath the skin.

Coop's eyes skittered over Alice, but he didn't comment on her disheveled appearance. His sneer was bitter. "You gonna say I'm not a Spencer too?"

He'd heard Leo's words. She felt the echo of his hurt, but she was hurt too. "Can't you stay clear of trouble just once?"

The bugle's call pierced the morning air, signaling departure.

Maddie appeared as if summoned, ready to drive the wagon with the boys. Coop stared at her. They were at an impasse. He pushed away from the wagon and stalked off without another word.

Alice stood there alone, snowflakes melting in her hair, watching her family fall apart piece by piece. The pain in her jaw was nothing compared to the ache in her chest as she realized she was losing her brother.

* * *

Rob heard everything—every harsh word Leo had thrown at Alice, every bitter response from Coop. Frustration and anger coursed through him like fire, made worse by his inability to move faster, to rescue Alice himself. Why couldn't the brothers see how their conflict was destroying the woman who loved them both?

Alice had turned away from Maddie and Belle, who had finally emerged from the wagon. Only when Rob shifted his weight on his crutch was Alice's attention caught. She looked up, surprised to find him still standing there. She wasn't crying, but her face was pale and drawn.

"We need to get you into the wagon," she said, her voice carefully controlled. "Everyone is rolling out."

Wagons were indeed moving past them, their wheels creaking and harnesses jingling as the company began its daily march. But Rob saw the fragile composure Alice was barely maintaining.

"Let's just take a minute," he said gently. "I want to make sure you're all right."

That simple kindness was her undoing. Her face crumpled like paper thrown into a fire, and a sob broke free before she could stop it.

Rob took a wobbling step toward her, making sure to keep his grip on his crutch this time. Alice moved toward him at the same moment, and suddenly she was burrowing into him, her face pressed against his chest as tears soaked through his shirt.

He let his free arm come around her, holding her as tightly as he dared, pressing his jaw against the top of her head. Her hair smelled like lavender and wood smoke, and he could feel the way her shoulders shook with each sob.

Anger spiraled through him—white-hot fury at her brothers for their blindness. He wished he could use his fists to beat some sense into Coop, to shake Leo until he realized what his harsh words were doing to his sister. Alice was the heart of their family, the one who had held them together after their mother died, and they were too caught up in their own pride to see they were breaking her.

But as her tears continued to wet his shirt, as he felt her lean into him—really lean on him for the first time since this whole journey had begun—a different realization struck him.

This wasn't about Coop's reckless choices or Leo's stubborn pride. It wasn't even about Rob's own desire to win Alice's heart. This was about Alice, and what Alice needed.

More wagons rolled past them, their occupants too focused on the day's travel to pay attention to the drama unfolding at the edge of camp. Alice pulled back slightly, worry creasing her brow.

"We're going to be left behind," she whispered, but Rob tightened his hold on her.

"There's plenty of time," he murmured against her hair. "This—being here with you in this moment—is the only thing that matters."

And he meant it. He'd been looking at everything all wrong, hadn't he? He'd been so focused on convincing Alice that they belonged together, so determined to overcome her objections and win her acceptance of his suit, that he'd missed what was right in front of him.

Alice was trying to hold her family together. After what she'd shared about losing her mother, about praying desperately for God to spare the woman who held their world together, Rob understood the fear that drove her now. She was terrified of losing another piece of her family, terrified that Coop's reckless choices would get him killed or cast out forever.

She didn't need Rob to convince her that Coop was a lost cause. She didn't need him to argue that her brothers didn't deserve her loyalty. She needed someone on her side—someone who would help her reconnect with her family, help keep Coop in line, help bridge the growing chasm between her brothers.

It wasn't about Coop. It wasn't about Leo. It wasn't even about Rob.

It was about Alice.

Another wagon passed, and Alice stirred in his arms, clearly worried about the time. But Rob held her steady, letting her take whatever comfort she could from his presence. The warmth of her against him, the trust it represented was worth more than all the pursuing and persuading he'd been doing.

Finally, Alice pulled away, wiping at her eyes with the back of her hand. Rob reached into his pocket and offered her his handkerchief.

"Thank you," she murmured, using it to dab at her face. She ducked her head. "I must look all splotchy."

"You're always beautiful," he said simply, meaning every word.

A faint flush crept into her cheeks despite her tears, but as she stepped back slightly, Rob's attention caught on something that made his chest tighten. An angry red scrape along her jaw and a bruise was already blooming beneath it, darkening the delicate skin.

Another rush of anger surged through him—not the hot, impulsive fury of moments ago, but something colder and more determined. Her brother had walked away without even checking to see if she was hurt.

"Let me see to that wound," he said, keeping his voice gentle despite the anger simmering beneath.

"It's fine, really." Alice's hand went automatically to her jaw, as if she could hide the injury.

"Alice, let me take a look."

She tried to wave him off, already turning toward the wagon, but when she took that first step, a wince flickered across her face—brief but unmistakable. Rob's hand shot out to catch her arm, steadying both of them.

"Where else are you hurt?"

"My side is just a little tender." She wouldn't quite meet his eyes. "It's nothing."

"Alice—"

She glanced up at him then, and something in her expression softened. "Don't look like that."

"Look like what?"

"Like you're going to punish someone."

Rob couldn't help the rueful smile that tugged at his mouth. He gestured down at himself—at the crutch, the splinted leg, the way he had to shift his weight carefully just to stay upright. "If only I was in the condition to do so."

He insisted she come along as he hobbled over to his wagon, each step requiring careful balance. Fortunately, there was a jar of antiseptic within reach at the back. Doc had been using it liberally on Rob's own injury. He poured some of the clear liquid onto the handkerchief Alice had just used to dry her tears.

"I can do it myself," Alice protested, reaching for the cloth.

Rob held it just out of her reach. "It's my turn to do the doctoring."

He lifted the dampened handkerchief toward her face, moving slowly to give her time to pull away if she truly didn't want this. But she stayed still, watching him with those luminous eyes that had haunted him since the moment he'd first truly seen her.

When the antiseptic touched the scraped skin, she inhaled sharply, a hiss of pain that made him wince in sympathy.

"I'm sorry," he murmured, keeping his touch as gentle as possible while cleaning the wound. "I know it stings."

For a moment, she let him be the one to take care of her. Let him carefully dab at the scrape, checking to make sure there was no dirt embedded in the broken skin. The intimacy of the moment—standing so close he could see the gold flecks in her eyes, could feel the warmth of her breath—filled him with a sense of affection so deep it almost hurt. An urge to protect her.

When he lowered his hand, Alice stepped back. The careful distance she maintained told him she'd felt it too—that pull between them that grew stronger every time they were close.

She couldn't quite hold his eyes, her gaze skittering away. "Thank you."

She glanced toward the moving wagons again, and he could see her pulling herself back together, rebuilding the walls she'd let down for those few precious moments.

"Let's get you into the wagon or we'll be left behind."

But as she moved to help him, Rob stopped her with a gentle touch to her arm.

"Alice, wait."

She looked up at him, and he saw the exhaustion in her eyes, the weight of responsibility she carried for everyone around her.

"I promise to stop pressuring on you to accept my suit."

He saw the flare of surprise in her eyes, followed quickly by something else. Vulnerability? He smiled, hoping to reassure her.

"My feelings haven't changed," he said carefully. "But perhaps what you need most right now is a friend. And I want to be that for you."

Eleven

THE CREEK WATER was blessedly cold against Alice's skin as she carefully patted her face, avoiding the tender bruise that had bloomed along her jaw. Even the gentlest touch made her wince, a sharp reminder of yesterday's fight.

Yesterday. When everything had changed.

She dipped her washcloth in the creek again, wringing it out before pressing it gingerly to her neck. She shivered when a drop of the icy water ran down her neck. Around her, the other women were spread out along this secluded bend in the creek —Rachel with baby Molly secured in a wrap against her chest, Felicity helping young Ben wash behind her ears, Evangeline keeping hold of Sarah's arm as the toddler attempted to jump into the shallows, and Belle hovering at the edge of the group, still skittish as a doe.

None of them had fully undressed. This wasn't a proper bath—just a hurried washing up before the company pulled out for the day. They used washcloths to clean what they could, staying mostly clothed for modesty and warmth in the crisp morning air and icy water.

Ever since yesterday, when Coop had gotten into that fight with those two men, something had shifted between her and Rob. There was a tenderness in the way he looked at her now, in the careful way he'd cleaned her wound. But his voice echoed in her mind too: *I promise to stop pressuring you to accept my suit.*

The words should have brought relief. Instead, they stirred up a confusion she didn't know how to untangle.

"Are you all right?"

Alice looked up to find Evangeline watching her with concern, little Sarah clinging to her mother's skirts with wet hands.

"I don't know," Alice admitted quietly. She'd scarcely slept last night for thinking over what had happened with her brothers—Leo's harsh dismissal, Coop's bitter words, the widening chasm between them that she seemed powerless to bridge.

Evangeline's expression softened with sympathy. "Leo will come around."

But Alice wasn't so sure. She shook her head slowly, feeling the ache in her jaw with the movement. "I've never seen him so furious with Coop. So... closed off."

A few feet away, Felicity was focused intently on helping Ben scrub her arms, but Alice could tell by the stillness of her posture that she was listening. Something in the set of Felicity's shoulders reminded Alice that August was dealing with a lot too. Since August's injury, things had changed between him and Felicity. Alice had noticed it in the careful distance Felicity maintained, the way August's jaw would tighten when his wife tried to help him with tasks he could no longer do alone.

"How are you, Felicity?" Alice asked gently. "How is August holding up?"

Felicity's hands stilled on Ben's arm for a moment. When she looked up, her expression was carefully neutral, but Alice could see the worry in her eyes.

"He seems to have a streak of the same stubbornness your brothers have," Felicity said quietly. "He's pushing me away. Won't let me help him, won't talk to me about what he's feeling." She turned her attention back to Ben, but her movements were mechanical. "I know he's hurting. I just... I don't know how to reach him anymore."

Alice opened her mouth, searching for words of comfort or wisdom, but found none. What could she say? That families were complicated? That the men they loved were stubborn and prideful? That sometimes love wasn't enough to bridge the distance grief and fear created?

Before she could formulate any response, the smell of wood smoke drifted on the breeze, and Rachel lifted her head, frowning. "Do you smell that?"

Alice inhaled deeply. Smoke, definitely. They'd walked a fair piece from camp, following the creek downstream for privacy, until the sounds of the company had faded to nothing. So the smoke couldn't be coming from the fires within their circled wagons. "It's not coming from the camp."

Belle's eyes went wide with panic. "It's him. It's Sarge." Her voice was barely audible. "He's going to kill all of us!"

Alice noticed the young woman's hand had snuck into her pocket. Wasn't that where she carried a knife?

Belle took a wavering step. "We have to run. Now."

"Hold on." Rachel shifted Molly in her wrap, reaching out to touch Belle's shoulder, but the young woman jerked away.

Felicity had already retrieved the rifle they'd brought with them, holding it pointed at the ground. "Let's not panic. It could be anyone."

Ben watched wide-eyed.

"Could be another company. I'll go find out," Alice said, already wringing out her washcloth and tucking it into her apron pocket.

"No!" Belle's voice cracked.

Rachel caught Belle's hands, holding them firmly. "If it was Sarge, he wouldn't have lit a fire, would he? If he was trying to sneak up on our company, he'd be trying to stay hidden."

Belle blinked at the clear logic.

"I'll come with you," Felicity said to Alice. Then she glanced at Rachel. "Can you watch over Ben?"

Rachel nodded, drawing Ben close to her side. "We'll head back to camp. Alert Owen and the others." Evangeline and Sarah stood, ready to join them.

Alice and Felicity moved through the woods, leaving the creek behind. Alice tried to place each footstep quietly, avoiding dried leaves and loose stones, just in case. Around them, the forest hummed with life—the chittering of squirrels in the branches overhead, the distant call of a jay, the whisper of wind through pine needles. Surely if animals sensed danger they would be quiet too.

A branch snapped under Felicity's boot, the crack loud enough to make Alice jump.

"Sorry," Felicity murmured.

They crept forward more slowly, and soon Alice heard voices—men's voices—carrying through the trees. Her pulse spiked. Belle had said Sarge was alone, hadn't she? This couldn't be him.

"Maybe it's another caravan." Felicity's voice, barely audible.

"Wouldn't the scouts have noticed?" But even as Alice whispered the question, she saw the way Felicity's face fell. August would never have let anyone sneak up on their camp. But August couldn't scout the way he used to, not since the accident.

The voices grew clearer as they edged closer to the source of the smoke.

"Whatever it was, it ripped into that ox like it was nothing." The man speaking seemed agitated.

"We have to find out what it was and kill it," a second voice responded, and something about the timbre of it tugged at Alice's memory. She knew that voice. Or thought she did.

Alice was just opening her mouth to tell Felicity when a rough voice barked from directly behind them.

"Stick 'em up."

They whirled to find a grizzled man pointing a rifle at them, his face hard beneath the shadow of his hat brim.

Alice's stomach dropped. The barrel of that rifle looked impossibly large, a dark circle of threat. Her heart hammered so hard against her ribs she could hear the pulse in her ears.

They'd gotten themselves into trouble. Real trouble. She'd been so focused on protecting Belle, on investigating the smoke, that she hadn't considered they might be walking into danger themselves. What if this man pulled that trigger?

Felicity shifted closer, her shoulder brushing Alice's, a small gesture of solidarity that steadied her slightly.

"Move it," the man ordered, gesturing with the gun barrel for them to go toward the clearing where the other voices were coming from. "Both of you."

"We mean no harm," Alice said quickly, raising her hands. Beside her, Felicity held her own rifle pointed carefully at the ground, non-threatening.

"I don't care. Don't wanna hear it." The man spat to the side. "Maybe you two are the ones who killed the boss's ox."

"The boss?" Alice asked, but the man cut her off.

"Shut up. Move."

He hadn't asked Felicity to drop her gun, and she continued to keep it pointed at the ground. She stuck right by Alice's side, their arms laced together.

"What kind of animal is big enough to kill an ox?" Felicity said under her breath.

Alice didn't want to think about it.

He herded them at gunpoint through the trees. As the woods opened up, Alice counted four wagons parked in a square and several men milling about. Most looked to be hands —cowboys or hired drivers.

And then she saw him.

A gray-haired man stood near the largest wagon, his back straight despite his years, his bearing unmistakable even from a distance. He turned at the sound of their approach, and Alice's breath caught in her throat.

Old Man Braddock. Rob's grandfather. Her former employer. The man she'd worked for in that grand house back in New Jersey.

* * *

The morning air bit cold against Rob's face as he made his way toward the cowboys' camp, his crutch sinking slightly into the frosty earth with each step. The camp was set apart from the main circle of wagons—just a collection of bedrolls scattered around a dying fire, with horses being saddled nearby. A couple of cowboys glanced up at his approach, their expressions curious but not unfriendly, before turning back to their work.

Coop was hunched down by the fire, poking at the embers with a stick. He looked up as Rob's shadow fell across him, and his expression immediately turned suspicious.

"Hullo," Rob offered.

Coop didn't respond, just watched him with narrowed eyes.

The other cowboys were preparing their horses for the day, checking cinches and adjusting stirrups in preparation for moving out with the cattle. Rob's attention caught on Coop's mount, a bay gelding that was shifting its weight oddly.

"Your horse looks like it's favoring one foot," Rob said, nodding toward the animal. "Might want to check that out before you ride."

Coop stood abruptly, planting his hands on his hips. Rob leaned heavily on his crutch, the package he'd brought tucked under his other arm.

"What do you want?" Coop demanded.

"I want to make nice. For Alice's sake."

Coop's eyebrows shot up in obvious disbelief.

Rob pressed on. "I've noticed you've been trying to talk to that young lady. Belle."

Coop bristled like a dog with its hackles raised. "You stay out of my business."

He took a step toward Rob, aggressive in his posture. But Rob didn't cower or step back. He held Coop's glare steadily. Coop wasn't going to knock him down. Hopefully.

"We both know if you actually meant me harm, you would have left me in that river."

The words hung in the air between them, and the moment they left Rob's mouth, a realization crashed over him. It was true. A memory hit him like a physical blow—pain so intense it had nearly knocked him unconscious, the icy bite of water stealing his breath, and Coop. Coop scrambling down the rocky riverbank, hands gripping under Rob's armpits, hauling him out of the current with desperate strength.

When Rob blinked back into the present, Coop's eyes had narrowed quizzically, as if he was trying to work out what Rob wanted.

Rob shifted the package from under his arm and extended it toward Coop. "This is a shawl I brought west." For Alice, but he didn't say that. "Belle's looks almost threadbare—full of holes. Winter's coming on. She's going to need something warm."

Coop's jaw jutted out stubbornly, but he didn't take the package.

"I know you've got some coins in your pocket from playing cards with the cowboys," Rob added.

For a long moment, Coop just glared at him. Long enough for him to wonder whether he'd made a mistake. Then Coop stomped over to his saddlebag, fished out some coins, and strode back to exchange it with Rob for the package.

"That wasn't so hard, was it?" Rob said mildly.

Before Coop could retort, shouts erupted from the direction of the main camp. Two women came running out of the woods, talking fast and gesturing wildly. Coop and one of the other cowboys jogged off to meet them.

Rob watched as Leo appeared, his expression tight as he joined the group. But Rob's attention had already shifted to two more figures emerging from the woods behind the women—Alice and Felicity, flanked by a man with silver hair that caught the morning light.

Rob's body went rigid. His breath stopped in his chest.

Leo barked something at Coop—sharp and dismissive. Coop bristled, but made his way back to his horse. Rob barely noticed, staring at the older man.

It couldn't be. But it was.

His grandfather.

Rob's heart leaped with joy at seeing his grandfather, but even in that moment of recognition, he caught the way Grandfather's gaze tracked Coop's departing figure. As Coop ducked behind the horse to check its hoof, the older man scowled.

Of course he'd recognize Coop.

Rob's stomach knotted. He hadn't forgotten the trouble Coop had caused at the mill—the explosion, the two men who'd died, the building that had been destroyed. Neither would Grandfather. The scowl remained on his grandfather's features as he moved to meet Rob.

Grandfather's commanding presence was unchanged despite the wilderness setting. But before Rob could formulate a coherent thought about what this meant—Grandfather here,

Grandfather having seen Coop—strong arms wrapped around him in an embrace.

The familiar smell hit him first—pipe tobacco and bay rum, the scent that had meant home for as long as Rob could remember. The breadth of his grandfather's shoulders, the strength in his grip, brought a wave of emotion so powerful that Rob had to clear his throat against the tightness building there.

When his grandfather stepped back, his hands still gripping Rob's shoulders, his eyes swept over Rob's injury with sharp assessment.

"What happened to you?"

"An accident." Rob's eyes involuntarily flicked over to meet Alice's. She stood a few paces back, her face pale, that bruise still visible on her jaw.

"We're pulling out soon," Leo called. His tone suggested he wasn't thrilled about the delay.

Rob's leg was beginning to throb from standing so long. Alice must have noticed, because she moved forward and murmured, "You should sit down. I can make a fresh pot of coffee for you both."

His grandfather walked beside him as Rob made his slow way back toward the campfire. As they moved through the camp, Rob became acutely aware of his grandfather's gaze sweeping over the circled wagons, the weary travelers packing up their belongings.

He'd grown so used to the group, it was a shock to see them through his grandfather's eyes. Would Grandfather notice the ragged state of Collin and Stella's wagon? The patched canvas and worn wheels had survived an ambush, but Grandfather wouldn't know. Would he see the family camped nearby—their threadbare clothing making it obvious they'd left home with little to their name?

Rob could almost feel his grandfather's judgment settling over these people, these travelers who had nothing in common with his wealthy circles back in New Jersey.

They settled by the fire, Rob lowering himself carefully onto a crate while his grandfather remained standing, that commanding presence impossible to ignore, as he stared at Rob's wagon.

"What are you doing here, Grandfather?" Rob finally asked.

His grandfather's expression hardened, his mouth pressing into a thin line. When he spoke, his voice carried that familiar tone of command—the one that had always made Rob's hackles rise. "I came to fetch you home after you abandoned the family, after you walked out without a thought."

Rob's jaw tightened, as his grandfather's words hit him like a physical blow, stealing his breath. *Abandoned. Walked out without a thought.*

As if Rob hadn't spent his whole life being told what to do, where to work, who to become. As if leaving hadn't been the only way to prove he was more than just an extension of his grandfather's will.

$$Twelve$$

ROB CAUGHT Alice's glance from where she stood pouring coffee into two tin mugs, her movements careful and practiced. But the moment their eyes met, Rob quickly cut his gaze away, facing his grandfather squarely.

"I explained everything in my letter," he said, keeping his voice steady despite the turmoil in his chest. "I want to make my own fortune, out here in the West."

Alice approached with the coffee. Rob couldn't help the burn in his face, and he accepted his mug with a quiet, "Thank you."

Grandfather simply took his own mug as if it were his right to be served, not even acknowledging Alice's presence. The casual dismissal rankled Rob, but he couldn't address it now—not with everything else hanging between them.

Grandfather's sneer was loaded with disdain.

Alice moved away, withdrawing to a spot just out of

earshot but still within sight. Rob was grateful for the small mercy of her not having to listen to what was coming.

"You know I've worked my whole life to make the Braddock Powder Mills what it is today," Grandfather said, "You're meant to carry on that legacy."

"That's your legacy," Rob countered. "I want something else."

Grandfather's gaze swept across the circled wagons, the worn canvas covers and patched wheels, the travelers moving about their morning tasks. His lip curled slightly. "This is no way to live."

Heat flared in Rob's chest. "The men on this wagon train have fought hard and worked together, used their brains to get us this far on the journey. They are good men."

Grandfather's expression shifted, becoming more calculating. "What about your cousins? Your duty to the family isn't only in operating the mills, but maintaining the wealth that the family depends on."

A bad taste filled Rob's mouth. "Maybe one of the girls will marry someone interested in continuing the legacy of the mill. Or running it."

Grandfather's cheeks mottled red beneath his silver mustache. He stood abruptly, his crate toppling to the ground. "No one else knows the mill like you do."

The memory flashed unbidden—Rob at fifteen, standing in the mill with sawdust clinging to his clothes, Grandfather's hand heavy on his shoulder. *You need to learn the ins and outs of this place, boy. Every wheel, every gear. It's your duty as a Braddock.*

"I'm not asking for your approval," Rob said, his voice

harder than he'd intended. "I never thought I would leave, but I've come to care—"

"Yes," Grandfather interrupted, his voice sharp as a blade. "You said in your letter you fancy yourself in love. With one of the housemaids."

The condescension in his tone made Rob's hands fist at his sides. This was exactly why he'd had to leave. Grandfather couldn't see him as anything other than a piece to be moved on his chessboard.

"That's not all she is." Thankfully out of her earshot.

"That girl isn't worthy of you, Rob." Grandfather's words came fast and cutting. "She's nothing more than a distraction, a fleeting fancy. You have responsibilities, a legacy to uphold."

"If you'd just listen—"

"Enough of this foolishness. It's time for you to come home. I've brought enough supplies for us to make a crossing back over the Rockies and start on the journey home."

"I won't."

Grandfather's face turned an even deeper shade of red.

The bugle's call pierced the morning air, signaling departure.

Collin appeared around the corner of the wagon, tipping his hat at Grandfather with exaggerated politeness, though his jaw was set firm. He'd clearly overheard at least some of what had been said. Rob welcomed the interruption.

"Would you like a hand up into the wagon?" Collin asked Rob, his tone carefully neutral.

"Yes. I'm actually feeling up to driving the wagon from the bench today."

Collin's eyebrow cocked slightly—a gesture Grandfather

couldn't see from his angle. Collin was obviously surprised, but he played along smoothly.

"We're getting ready to pull out," Collin said to Grandfather with cool dismissal. "You'll want to make sure you're out of the way of the wagons."

"I'm not finished speaking to my grandson," Grandfather insisted.

"We're done for now." Rob met his grandfather's glare without flinching. "This is my wagon, and I'm driving it today."

For a long moment, Grandfather looked as if he might argue further. Then he turned on his heel and stalked away toward his own camp.

Collin helped Rob lever himself up onto the wagon bench. Despite his best efforts, he couldn't suppress a sharp intake of breath when his leg jarred against the seat. Pain lanced through his thigh, white-hot and intense.

Alice appeared as Rob was settling himself, her eyes widening slightly in surprise to find him on the bench instead of lying in the wagon bed.

"Would you ride with him for a bit?" Collin suggested before Rob could speak. "Just in case he needs help."

Alice hesitated, then nodded and climbed up to sit beside Rob.

Once Collin had moved away, Rob clucked the oxen into motion, the reins loose in his hands. "I'm sorry. Grandfather was rude to you."

Her chin lifted slightly, stubbornly. "I didn't notice a difference," she said quietly, without malice. "He's the same as he always is."

Her words settled in his chest with uncomfortable weight, reminding him of how he'd felt when he realized he hadn't even noticed Alice for years back in New Jersey. He'd been following in his grandfather's footsteps in that manner for far too long.

The wagons began rolling out, one by one finding their place in the line. Rob took up the long whip used to prod the oxen forward, calling out the command. The animals leaned into their yokes, and the wagon lurched into motion. It wasn't comfortable, these feelings battling inside him.

Rob kept his eyes on the horizon, the familiar landscape of rolling hills and distant mountains. "After my parents died, when I was young, I looked up to Grandfather like a father figure. Always respected him."

It hung unspoken in the air between them that something was changing.

"When I was about ten," Rob continued, partly to distract himself from the throbbing in his leg, "I witnessed Grandfather calm a riot at the mill. Some of the men were demanding—" He paused, trying to remember. "I don't really recall what it was about, but there was a crowd of them. Angry."

Alice was listening, her attention fully on him even as she kept one eye on the rocky trail ahead.

"I was so frightened when that group of men pushed their way into the main house that I hid in one of the closets downstairs, in the servant's hallway." The memory was vivid even now—the darkness of that cramped space, the smell of the coats hung there, his heart hammering with terror. "Through the door, I watched Grandfather calm them. He didn't back down, didn't show fear. He gave orders. And they listened."

His leg spasmed, and he winced. Alice noticed immediately, reaching for the whip. "Let me," she said softly.

He handed it over, grateful.

"I wanted to be just like him," Rob admitted. "I knew I'd been a coward, hiding like that. So I vowed I'd do everything I could to become like my grandfather."

Alice was quiet for a moment, the only sounds the creaking of the wagon and the steady plod of the oxen's hooves. When she spoke, her voice was thoughtful.

"There are different types of leadership, you know. Jesus led his disciples and washed their feet. He led others, he didn't control them." She glanced at him, and something gentled in her expression. "From what Leo says, when you worked in the mill with him, you were a good leader for the other men."

Rob turned to look at her fully, surprised. He'd expected... well, he wasn't sure what he'd expected. But not this quiet affirmation, not this recognition of something he'd barely recognized in himself.

The surprise must have shown on his face, because a faint flush crept into Alice's cheeks and she turned her attention back to the oxen. But her words settled into him, taking root in places that had been waiting for something other than his grandfather's shadow.

Only hours later, Alice's hands were slick as she plucked feathers from the small bird she held, her fingers working with practiced efficiency despite the dampness that clung to everything.

A fog had rolled in, growing thicker over the past hour, wrapping the mountainside in a damp, blinding shroud. It hadn't taken long for Hollis to call the company to halt, the scout having warned of treacherous terrain ahead—hidden depressions and possibly caves, too dangerous to navigate without full visibility. Now the wagons huddled together like hulking statues in the gloom, and an uneasy quiet had settled over the camp.

Mist clung to Alice's skin, and the air was thick with the scent of damp earth and the faint metallic tang of the game she was preparing. Stella sat on a crate nearby, darning a sock. Around them, other travelers moved about their tasks, their forms ghostly in the fog.

Seeing Rob's grandfather—somehow she couldn't quite use the nickname *Old Man* that the other servants and mill workers had used, tongue in cheek, back in New Jersey—this morning had been abrupt and a little surreal, like stepping back into a life she'd thought she'd left behind. For a moment, walking back into camp with him and his men, she'd felt like a housemaid again, invisible except when needed. It had settled into something familiar, something she'd known for years: his belief that she was less-than, beneath notice unless she was being useful.

What surprised her was how much it stung now. After these weeks spent with Rob, after the way he looked at her—as if he truly saw her—the casual dismissal cut deeper than it used to. It shouldn't have mattered. She'd known for years what the Braddocks thought of her. But somehow, it did matter.

"You've been quiet today," Stella said, her voice soft but probing. "Collin told me what Rob's grandfather said about you. It sounds like the men who ran the factory I worked at in Dublin." She kept her eyes on her handiwork, squinting down at the toe of the sock. "Knowing he thinks of his employees that way is different than knowing he thinks so low of you."

Alice's breath caught painfully. She exhaled through her nose. What could she do about it? Nothing.

She plucked the next feathers with more force. "I shouldn't care. I've known how he thinks of his employees for years. I'm surprised he even knows my name."

Stella hesitated, then asked, "Do you think Rob will go back to New Jersey?"

The question landed like a stone in Alice's chest. She shrugged, but the motion felt stiff, forced. The thought of Rob leaving stabbed at her—a sharp pain she hadn't expected and didn't want to examine too closely. It was silly, she told herself. She'd made it clear to him that their relationship couldn't be anything more than friendship.

Stella watched Alice, probably seeing too much. Then she put her sock and needle back in her lap, shifting on the crate. Alice couldn't help but notice the pain lines around her mouth.

"Here, let me help you back to the wagon so you can rest." Alice stood and brushed feathers from her apron.

The fact that her sister-in-law didn't argue said a lot about her pain. After Alice helped Stella back into the wagon and was urged away due to too much fussing, she stood beside the wagon, looking into the swirling fog. It seemed to swallow everything, muffling the sounds all around her and making her feel small and isolated.

Sudden movement made her jump. Someone was approaching from outside the camp.

"What will it take to get you to release your claim on my grandson?"

The voice startled her so badly she nearly dropped her knife. Rob's grandfather stood there, his figure blurred by the mist. His tone was accusatory and disdainful—the same tone he'd used with servants who'd displeased him. "Money? Jewels?"

Alice's grip tightened on the bird, her fingers ripping at feathers with more force than necessary. "I have no claim on your grandson."

"He left me a letter," the old man said, his voice dripping with condescension. "A letter to tell me he'd fallen in love with you before he abandoned his family home and everything he values. You've turned his head with your pretty face, but you're not of his station, and I won't stand for it."

Alice's heart lurched painfully. *Fallen in love?* Rob couldn't have written those words. He'd never said anything like that to her. Her mind raced back to their last real conversation, when he'd told her he wouldn't push for them to be together anymore, that he wanted to be her friend. Had his feelings been different before they'd left New Jersey? Or was his grandfather twisting Rob's words to suit his own purposes? To manipulate her?

"You're reaching above your station," the old man continued, his voice cold. "How dare you—a simpleton, a maid—try and tempt my grandson? You think you're better than you are."

The words hit differently than they would have months ago. Back in New Jersey, she'd learned to let such comments slide off her like water, to make herself small and invisible. But now, after Rob had treated her as an equal, after he'd listened to her thoughts and valued her opinions, the dismissal burned.

Alice stood, feathers flying from her apron as she rose to face him. She didn't close the distance between them, but she met his gaze steadily. "I know exactly who I am. I know exactly my station, and I've been telling your grandson that we will never suit."

The old man's lips curled into a sneer. "I'm surprised you have a lick of sense. I wouldn't have expected it."

Heat flooded Alice's face, and her temper flared at his assumption, his rude words. "If your grandson offered for my hand, it would be my choice whether or not to accept it. Only mine."

Over the old man's shoulder, she saw Rob's head and shoulders emerge from the fog. He hobbled into the clearing, his face white with anger, his eyes flicking between Alice and his grandfather.

"How dare you speak to her like that."

"Rob—"

Two gunshots cracked through the fog.

Alice jumped, her heart leaping into her throat. A shout echoed from somewhere in the circle of wagons, and then Stella's voice pierced the air.

"Collin!"

For a frozen moment, Alice couldn't move. Had someone shot at Collin?

Then Rob was there, hobbling toward her with determined, uneven steps. He positioned himself between her and the woods, shielding her despite his injury.

"Get down," he urged.

Alice's arm came instinctively around his waist, helping support him as they moved toward the wagons. "You're in no shape to go after anyone who's out there," she said.

Rob's grandfather pressed close behind them. The fog seemed to close in around them, reducing the world to the small circle huddled near the wagons.

For a moment, Alice's gaze clashed with Rob's, seeing something in the depths of his eyes that she couldn't face right now. Her heart pounded so hard she could barely breathe.

What had happened to Collin? Where was Coop? Where was Leo?

"Belle, don't!" Coop's shout rang out through the fog.

Rob pressed Alice closer to the wagon, his body a shield despite his injured leg. Around them, the fog grew deeper, swirling in thick tendrils that obscured everything. Voices called out—panicked, confused, searching—but the mist made it impossible to tell where anyone was or what was happening.

Alice clung to Rob's solid presence.

Was someone attacking the train—or just her family?

Thirteen

THE HEAVY FOG had descended like a suffocating blanket, and Belle couldn't explain it, but she knew Sarge was close. The certainty of it made her skin crawl, made every shadow in the mist look like a threat.

She'd been hiding in Doc and Maddie's wagon all day, ever since the scare at the creek that morning when she'd been certain Sarge had caught up to her. The wagon had felt safe, cramped but safe, with Maddie corralling the children inside to keep them from wandering off and getting lost in the fog.

But now her throat was parched, her tongue sticky against the roof of her mouth. The water pail hung just outside the wagon. She could see it through the gap in the canvas. Just a few steps. A quick dipper of water and she'd be back inside.

Belle pushed aside the canvas and climbed down carefully, her shoes—the ones Alice had given her, blessedly flat unlike the impractical heeled boots she'd worn at the fort—finding purchase on the damp ground. The dress Alice had given her rustled as she moved, and she pulled her threadbare shawl tighter around her shoulders against the chill. Her knife lodged a familiar weight in her pocket. She'd learned never to be without it.

She reached for the dipper with trembling hands.

Two gunshots cracked through the fog.

Belle's heart stopped. Shouts erupted from somewhere in the mist—panicked, angry, she couldn't tell. Two more shots followed, the sounds sharp and devastating.

Then she saw it—a flash of dark fabric, a man's pant leg appearing through the fog. Moving toward her. The body was indistinct, just a shadow in the mist, but it was coming her direction.

Her fear expanded until it was all she knew. Her pulse hammered so hard she could hear it in her ears. Her hands shook, and she dropped the dipper. She couldn't let anything happen to the children. Or to Maddie, who'd done so much for her, hidden her and protected her when she had no right to expect kindness from anyone.

Belle dropped the dipper and ran.

A shout rang out behind her—her name, maybe, though she couldn't recognize the voice through the roaring in her ears. She couldn't breathe. The fog wrapped around her like grasping hands, obscuring everything. The landscape on this rocky hillside was barren—no trees to hide behind, no shelter visible through the thick mist.

She needed shelter. An escape. But she found only more fog.

Someone followed behind her, making no effort to quiet their pounding steps. Catching up. Her breath came in gasps that burned her throat. The fear was choking her, a physical thing that squeezed her chest and made her vision narrow.

A hand grabbed the back of her skirt.

At the same moment, Belle's foot found nothing but air.

She fell into nothing, taking her attacker with her.

The sensation was sickeningly familiar—the lurch in her stomach, the helpless flailing of her arms. But this time she wasn't being shoved down stairs or thrown against a wall. This time there was nothing beneath her at all.

She could feel the man's weight behind her as they plummeted through darkness. Her hand found her knife, yanked it from her pocket with desperate instinct. She tried to twist away from him even as they fell through what felt like endless space.

He grunted.

He was much bigger than her.

They shifted as they fell, his body turning, and then—

Impact.

The breath slammed out of her lungs. But she'd landed on top of him, his body breaking her fall. It was pitch dark—not the fog's gray obscurity but complete, absolute darkness that pressed against her eyes.

He still had hold of the back of her dress. Belle pushed against his stomach with one hand, trying to get up, get away. He groaned, the sound pained, and his body shifted beneath her, almost toppling her.

She raised the knife. Had to get away. Had to—

The blade caught fabric, maybe a bit of skin on his arm. Not deep. Not what she'd been aiming for—his torso, his face, anywhere that would make him let go.

"It's me—Coop." The voice came from the darkness, strained with pain.

Through the pounding in her ears, Belle finally recognized it.

Coop Spencer.

He released his hold and Belle scrambled backward, her shoes scrabbling against rock and loose gravel. She didn't stop until her back and shoulders hit a wall. She gripped the knife in both hands, holding it out in front of her even though she couldn't see anything. Her ears strained to hear over the frantic beating of her heart.

He wasn't moving. Or was he? She couldn't tell in the darkness.

"Where are we?" Her voice came out tremulous.

She heard him moving then, though the sounds didn't seem to be coming closer. Fabric rustling. A grunt of pain.

"I think we fell into some kind of cave," Coop said.

Belle shook so badly that the rocks beneath her rattled, the sound unnaturally loud in the enclosed space. The memory of him intercepting those two men flashed through her mind—how he'd positioned himself between them and her, how he had fought them. But the moment fists had started flying, she'd been thrown back into memories of bar fights at the saloon, brawls that always ended with someone bleeding. All it would take was one fist to knock her down. She'd seen Alice get knocked down.

Coop was violent, unpredictable. She didn't know what he could do.

"Are you okay?" Coop asked.

"Just stay back," Belle snapped, her voice sharp.

A pause. "I'm gonna see if I can feel my way back up. See if we can get out the way we came."

She heard more movement—the scrape of boots on rock, heavy breathing. She remembered the blood on his face, the way he'd moved stiffly after the fight. Now there were grunts of effort, muffled in the darkness.

The seconds stretched into minutes. Belle stayed pressed against the wall, knife clutched in her hands, trying to track his location by sound alone. Her eyes ached from straining to see. The cave smelled of damp earth, like stone that had never seen sunlight. Somewhere in the distance, she thought she could hear the faint drip of water.

Finally, there was a thump. Coop's breathing grew louder. "It's no good. Bad angle. The rock's too slippery. I can't get any purchase."

Belle's chest locked with fresh panic. "Can we light a torch? It's really dark."

There were scrabbling sounds, as if he searched the ground.

Another pause. "I've got flint and steel in my pocket, but there's nothing to burn."

Before she could respond, he asked, "Are you wearing your shawl? Are you cold?"

The question was oddly specific. There was a tone in his voice she couldn't quite understand.

"The temperature's fallen over the last few hours," Coop continued. "We need all the clothing we're wearing. Can't light any of that."

Silence settled between them, broken only by Coop's gradually evening breathing. Belle stayed very still, aware of every sound, every shift in the air that might tell her where he was.

"Why did you run?" His voice came from the darkness, quieter now.

Belle's throat tightened. "I felt like Sarge was close."

"Why does he want you dead?"

The image flashed before her eyes—Pretty's hand flopping in the dirt, sticky with blood. The shivers got worse, Belle's whole body trembling despite the shawl.

"I saw him kill someone," she forced out through gritted teeth.

She couldn't say more than that. Couldn't speak Pretty's name, couldn't explain how Sarge had found out she'd witnessed his crime. She'd left almost immediately, hadn't even gone back into the saloon. How had he known?

Coop tried to lighten his tone. "Well, I guess one good thing is he's not gonna find you down here."

"What if no one else finds us?" The words came out smaller than Belle intended, the fear she'd been holding back creeping into her voice.

"My brothers won't leave without me."

But there was uncertainty in his tone, and Belle knew—everyone knew—that Coop didn't have a great relationship with his family. She'd overheard the arguments.

A longer silence. Then: "Help!" Coop's sudden shout startled her. His voice echoed up the tube they'd fallen through, bouncing back at them before seeming to echo deeper into the earth, the sound disappearing into unseen depths. He called out again and again.

No answer came from above.

"I think maybe we should explore," Coop said after a

moment. "See if there's another way out of here. I think I feel a breeze, maybe."

Belle's stomach dropped. She didn't want to go deeper into this suffocating darkness. But she also couldn't stay here alone. The thought of being abandoned in the pitch black made her chest constrict with panic. She might not hear if he snuck up on her again.

She heard him moving, heard the careful shuffle of his feet and the sound of his hands feeling along the wall. The cave must continue beyond where they'd landed, but there was no way to know.

Belle stayed pressed against her wall, turning her body to track his movements by sound. She sat in a protective position, knees drawn up, knife still gripped tightly in both hands. Every tiny noise made her flinch—the scatter of pebbles under his boots, the whisper of fabric against stone, his breathing.

She was stuck down here with this unpredictable man who'd gotten himself into a fistfight without a second thought. She didn't know what he might do to her. But her only other choice was to stay here alone in the darkness, and that thought terrified her almost as much as Sarge did.

"Come on," Coop said from somewhere ahead. "We need to find a way out."

Belle forced herself to her feet, her legs shaking. She had no choice but to follow him into the unknown depths of the cave.

* * *

"Where's Felicity?"

August turned his head toward Ben's voice. The gesture

was as automatic as it was useless. The fog had dampened every sound, muffling the camp noises he usually relied on to orient himself. Even Ben's voice seemed to come from everywhere and nowhere at once.

"She went to help Abigail," August said, keeping his voice calm. "She'll be back soon."

Four gunshots had rung out minutes ago—he'd counted them, his body tensing with each crack of gunfire. He'd brought Ben to huddle with him beneath the wagon. He felt helpless.

Which direction had the shots come from? It seemed impossible to pinpoint in the thick fog. Now the camp was filled with shouts and confusion, people calling for loved ones, trying to account for everyone.

"What if she's been shot?" Ben's voice climbed higher, edged with panic. "What if someone hurt her? What if—"

"Ben, it's all right." August reached in her direction, found her thin shoulder and squeezed gently. "Felicity's smart. She knows to stay close to the wagons."

But Ben was shaking under his hand, her breath coming in quick, frightened gasps. The ambush. August's breath locked in his chest as he realized what the sound of shots had brought up in her memories. The recent attack on their wagon train had brought it all back—the original ambush that had killed her parents, that had left her orphaned and terrified. And before that could fully heal, another attack. No wonder she was falling apart.

"Ben, listen to me—"

But she was already moving, pulling away from his grip. Her footsteps were muffled against the damp earth.

"Wait! Ben!" August lurched to his feet, his hand shooting out to try and catch her. His fingers closed on empty air.

"Help!" he called out. "Someone stop her!"

No one answered. The fog swallowed his voice, and he realized with sinking certainty that everyone nearby had scattered, called away by the gunshots and the chaos.

August had no choice. He couldn't let her run off alone in this fog, not with someone shooting, not with her in such a state of panic.

He started walking in the direction he thought she'd gone, his arms outstretched in front of him. The fog pressed against his face, cold and damp, obscuring what little light and shadow his damaged vision could detect. Before long, it cut off the sounds he relied on to orient himself—the creak of wagons, the voices of travelers, the stamp of oxen's hooves. Everything was muffled, distorted through the fog.

How far had he gone? He knew better than to keep going. Knew he should stop, call for help again, wait for someone to find him. But Ben was out there somewhere, frightened and alone. So he kept going.

August took another step. Then another.

His foot found nothing but air.

For one suspended moment, he was falling, his arms reaching uselessly. His hands scraped against rock as he tried to brace himself. His back slammed against rock walls. It was some kind of vertical shaft. Pain exploded along his spine. His rear hit another jutting rock, spinning him partially around as he continued to fall.

The smell of damp stone and earth filled his nose. The sound of his own body hitting rock echoed in the confined space, mixing with his gasping breaths. Cold air rushed past his face.

Then impact.

August hit the ground hard, the breath driven from his lungs. For a moment he could only lie there, stunned, his ribs screaming in protest. Slowly, he drew in a shaky breath. Then another.

He was alive.

His heart hammered in his ears, the only sound in the absolute stillness. August strained to hear anything else—footsteps above, voices, even the whisper of wind. But there was nothing. Just his own ragged breathing and the thunder of his pulse.

The cold bit through his clothes immediately. The fog had brought freezing temperatures, and down here, it was somehow worse. He could feel it seeping into his bones.

August pushed himself up to sitting, biting back a groan. His hands felt along the ground—rough stone, scattered with smaller rocks and gravel. He crawled forward, his palms scraping against the uneven surface, feeling for any opening, any passage that might lead somewhere.

His reaching hand hit solid rock. A wall.

He turned, crawling in a different direction. More rock. He kept moving, methodically checking every direction, his hands mapping out the space. It wasn't large. Maybe eight feet across at most. And everywhere he reached, he found walls.

Finally, his fingers encountered something different—larger rocks, piled against each other in what felt like a jumble of fallen stone. A cave-in. At some point, the passage had collapsed, sealing off whatever lay beyond.

There was no way out.

August sat back against the wall, his breath coming faster. He had to try to climb back up. Had to at least attempt it.

He turned toward where he'd fallen, reaching up to feel the walls of the shaft. They slanted inward slightly, rough enough that there might be handholds. August started to climb, moving quickly, his fingers finding purchase in cracks and on jutting rocks.

He made it a few feet—he thought it was a few feet, though he had no way to measure. Then the angle steepened sharply. His fingers scrabbled for grip, found nothing. His boots slipped.

August slid back down, the rock scraping the palms of his hands raw. He jarred his chin on the wall before he landed in a heap at the bottom, pain lancing through his already-bruised back.

He sat there, breathing hard, forcing himself to think. He was moving too fast. He needed to go slower, test each handhold before trusting his weight to it.

August started again, this time with agonizing care. He felt each crack, each protrusion, making sure it would hold before pulling himself up. Inch by painful inch, he climbed. The cold made his fingers stiff, harder to control.

How far had he climbed? How far still to go?

Then his hand closed on a section of rock that crumbled under his grip. For one terrible moment, he balanced on nothing. Then he was falling again, tumbling down the shaft and landing hard at the bottom with a cry he couldn't suppress.

August lay there, his body screaming with pain, his hands bleeding from the scrapes. The cold was worse now, seeping through his shirt, making him shiver.

He'd made a deadly mistake. He'd chased after Ben into the fog, and now he had no idea how far from camp he was. No one would know where he'd gone. No one would know to look for him.

Felicity's face rose in his mind, the way she must've looked at him two days ago when he'd said those words he couldn't take back. *Maybe we'd be better off if we weren't married.* He'd felt her hurt, even if he couldn't see her face.

He'd been angry, frustrated at his helplessness, at the way she tried to do everything for him as if he were a child. He'd wanted to hurt her, to make her understand how trapped he felt.

He'd succeeded.

She'd barely spoken to him since. They shared a tent, but she might as well have been a thousand miles away. She moved stiffly around him. Gone was her cheerful voice, the gentle touch that had felt like *home*. Until it didn't.

Why would she even look for him now? What good was he to anyone? A blind man who couldn't scout, couldn't protect his family, couldn't even keep track of a frightened little girl in the fog.

The cold pressed in from all sides, and August pulled his knees to his chest, trying to conserve warmth.

Maybe this was for the best. Maybe everyone would be better off if he just... stayed gone. One less burden for Felicity to carry. One less useless mouth to feed.

The darkness pressed against him, absolute and suffocating, and August closed his eyes against tears that no one would ever see.

Fourteen

ALICE COULDN'T SEEM to stop shaking.

Doc had just asked her to boil some water because Collin needed stitches. The bullet had missed him, ricocheting off some wood and lodging a splinter deep in his shoulder. Not serious, Doc had assured him quickly, but it needed cleaning and two or three stitches to close properly.

Minutes before that, Hollis had called for the wagons to be moved into a tighter circle. A more defensive one. Some of the men had gone out to search for whoever had been shooting.

Now Alice carried an armful of wood from the wagon toward the fire that was already burning. It needed to be bigger, hotter, to boil the water quickly. Her hands trembled as she added the wood piece by piece, and she couldn't steady them no matter how hard she tried. Rob sat nearby on the ground, using a crate as a makeshift work surface. He had his shoulder turned and she couldn't see what he was doing. She didn't mind. She didn't want to be distracted.

Through the fog—still thick but not as suffocating as before—she heard voices. Disembodied, impossible to pinpoint. Leo's voice, grim and low. Owen responding. Someone else she couldn't identify.

"—still no sign of them."

"Coop and Belle are both missing. August too."

A fourth voice joined the conversation. Maybe Gerry Bones, one of the other cowboys. "Mrs. Fletcher was near the edge of camp when the shots were fired. She said she saw a man. He fit the description of that fellow Belle's been hiding from. Dark hair, scar on his hand. Saw him clear as day raising his rifle toward Collin."

Alice positioned the water pot over the flames, then stoked the fire higher.

"You mind helping me?" Rob asked. "It won't take long."

She rose to go to him.

Out there somewhere, Owen spoke grimly. "If that's the same man who's been hunting Belle, he's still out there."

Leo made a disparaging noise, the sound carrying through the mist. "Knowing Coop, he's gotten himself into some romantic trouble instead of real trouble."

"You don't mean that." Owen's voice was sharp with reproach.

Silence followed, heavy with meaning.

A tear slipped down Alice's cheek before she could stop it. She quickly wiped it away with the back of her hand. Focused on Rob. He'd spread some kind of cloth over the top of the crate, and his hands were buried in what looked like dough. He watched her. Of course he'd seen her tears. But he didn't comment, and she was grateful for that small mercy.

"What are you doing?" she asked, her voice not quite steady.

"Making biscuits. Trying to." He said it with such chagrin that under other circumstances, it might have been funny.

Alice moved closer and saw the mess he'd made. The dough was far too sticky, clinging to his fingers in gluey clumps. It hadn't formed properly in the bowl he'd been using, and now dough smeared across the crate and his hands.

She had a few moments before her water would boil. She knelt beside him. Without asking, she reached for the flour sack and added several handfuls to his bowl, working it in with practiced motions. She helped him scrape the sticky mess off his hands, trying to ignore the sensation of touching him. Especially when his fingers curled naturally into her touch.

They both stared at their hands.

"I've watched you make biscuits about a dozen times since I was injured," Rob admitted, his voice husky. "It always looks so easy when you do it."

Alice showed him how to form the biscuits properly, pressing the dough into the waiting pans. He copied her movements.

"Why are you trying to make biscuits?" she asked.

Rob kept his eyes on the task. "They're likely going to send out search parties, aren't they? Men will be hungry when they come back."

She noticed for the first time that multiple pans sat on his crate—far more biscuits than would normally be needed for the Spencer crew. And there, in the pot, waiting, were the birds she'd skinned earlier.

"I didn't quite know what to do with the stew," he added quietly.

He'd been trying to help. Trying to ease her burden. For a moment, her breath caught in her throat.

All at once, emotion burst through Alice's carefully maintained composure. She stood up, turned away, pressed the back of her hand to her mouth. The fog still hung in patches around them. There was nowhere to go. Nowhere to hide.

She heard Rob slowly getting to his feet, the scrape of his crutch against the ground.

"Don't," she said, turning back toward him.

But he was already at her side.

His arms came around her, and Alice went into them without resistance. She let herself have this moment, pressing her cheek against his chest, feeling the steady beat of his heart beneath her ear. The tears came freely, and she didn't try to stop them.

Rob held her close, his hand coming up to cradle the back of her head. For this moment, she could let someone else carry the weight she'd been bearing alone.

He'd seen what she needed. Had chosen a task that would help her family. The realization made her chest ache with something too big to name.

"I'm sorry," she whispered against his shirt.

"Don't be." His voice rumbled through his chest, warm and close. "You have nothing to be sorry for."

His hand moved to the nape of her neck, his thumb stroking gently along the sensitive skin there. The touch sent warmth cascading down her spine, made her aware of the breadth of his chest against her cheek. The strength in his arms. The way his jaw rested lightly against the top of her head.

"Someone is going to find your brothers and bring them home safely."

The certainty in his voice steadied the fear inside her. She thought about what he'd said earlier in the day while sitting on the wagon bench beside her, about seeing his grandfather in a new light. Rob was a product of how he'd been raised, yes. But he was so much more than that.

Maybe she'd been wrong all this time. Maybe he was different from his grandfather. And maybe—just maybe—things could work between them.

The thought was terrifying and thrilling in equal measure.

Rob eased back slightly, and Alice felt the loss of his warmth. He brushed away a tear from her cheek, his touch gentle. He didn't try for a kiss, didn't press closer. He simply rested his forehead against hers for a moment before settling his jaw back on top of her head, holding her close.

"I'm sorry your brothers can't see that you need them," he murmured into her hair.

The words unlocked something inside her, and before she could stop herself, the truth came spilling out.

"I don't let them see that I need them."

Rob stilled, listening.

"When my stepfather died, I was nine years old." The words felt strange in her mouth, a story she'd never told anyone. "I was devastated. Grieving. Lost. I went to my mother because I needed her. I needed someone to tell me it would be all right."

Rob's hand resumed its gentle stroking at her nape, encouraging her to continue.

"But Mama couldn't see my grief. She looked at me and said, 'I'm going to have to go to work now. You're going to have to keep the household running.'" Alice's voice cracked slightly. "I was nine years old, and she needed me to be strong. To push aside what I was feeling and do what needed to be done."

"Alice..." Rob's voice was tight.

"I learned that day that my emotions didn't matter. That what I needed didn't matter. What mattered was taking care of everyone else." The tears came faster now. "So I never let them see. I never let anyone see."

Rob's arms tightened around her. It was a moment before he spoke. "That was a lot for a little girl to take on. I'm sorry that happened to you."

"It's just how things were." She tried to inject some strength into her voice. "It's what families do."

"But things are different now." His hand cupped her jaw, tilting her face up so she had to look at him. "Your brothers are grown. You did what your mother asked of you—more than she should have asked. But Alice, you don't have to carry that burden anymore."

The words stirred in her chest.

"God walked with you through all of that," Rob continued softly. "He saw you. Even when no one else did, He saw that little girl trying so hard to hold everything together. And He sees you now."

Alice's breath hitched. Had God walked with her through those hard years? It had felt so painful, so lonely. But maybe... maybe Rob was right. Maybe she hadn't been as alone as she'd felt.

"Your brothers are grown," Rob repeated. "And maybe they still can't see what you need. But I do."

The words hung between them, weighted with meaning. Alice's gaze dropped to where her hand rested against his chest, could feel his heartbeat steady and sure beneath her palm. When she looked back up, his eyes were warm with an emotion that made her pulse quicken.

"I don't want you to go back to New Jersey," she whispered.

A slow, tender smile spread across Rob's face. He pulled her close again, his embrace gentle but firm, and he pressed a kiss to the top of her head.

But he didn't give her an assurance he would stay.

Before the silence could stretch too long, Doc's voice called out from somewhere in the fog.

"Where's that water? And I need some clean cloths too!"

Alice pulled back reluctantly, and Rob let her go, though his fingers trailed down her arm as she stepped away, a touch that lingered even after contact was broken. Their eyes met one more time, and in that look, Alice saw everything he hadn't said aloud.

Then she turned and hurried to help Doc.

Belle woke with a start, her heart pounding.

Darkness. Complete and absolute. For a disorienting moment, she couldn't remember where she was, only that it was dark, and in the dark, anything could happen. Anyone could come through that door—

No. Not a door. A cave.

The memories rushed back. Falling through fog. Tumbling down into pitch blackness with Coop. Walking—sometimes crawling—through passages that never seemed to end. They'd traveled for hours, searching for an exit they never found.

How long had she slept?

She hadn't meant to sleep at all. She'd been leaning against the wall, her knife gripped tight in her hand. She must have drifted off.

The darkness still pressed against her, thick and suffocating, and Belle couldn't stop shivering. The cold had intensified while she slept, seeping through Alice's dress and her own threadbare shawl, settling into her bones until her teeth chattered.

She heard breathing in the darkness. Coop, somewhere close. Was he awake or asleep? She couldn't tell.

She didn't know what to make of him. She'd spent hours waiting for him to grab her. Touch her. Say something other than necessary instructions about their journey. *Watch your head. The passage gets tight here.* He'd barely spoken otherwise.

There was no one down here to know if he forced himself on her. Who would care, anyway?

She blinked herself out of her thoughts and shifted slightly, intending to pull her shawl tighter, and realized with a jolt of panic that her hand was empty.

The knife. Where was her knife?

She scrabbled frantically at the ground around her, her fingers scraping against rough stone and loose gravel. It had to be here.

"What's the matter?" Coop's voice came from the darkness, alert and calm despite how exhausted he must be.

Belle didn't answer, couldn't answer past the fear clogging her throat. She needed that knife. What if he grabbed her? She needed—

She tensed, sensing him moving closer in the darkness. Hearing the rustle of fabric and the scrape of his boots against stone. Then a metallic sound—the knife sliding across rock.

"Here." His hand found hers in the darkness, and their fingers connected as he pressed the knife handle into her palm. His touch was gentle, careful.

Belle's grip tightened on the knife the moment she had it back.

"You're freezing," Coop said quietly.

His hand touched her arm—just a light touch through the fabric of Alice's dress—and Belle flinched. But he was right. She was freezing. The shivers were getting worse, making her whole body tremble.

"There's nothing to make a fire with down here," Coop continued. "I think folks will be looking for us, but maybe they won't find us until morning. We've got to stay warm until then."

Was this the moment he would suggest a lewd way of keeping warm?

Belle gripped her knife tighter, her mind racing. Why hadn't she stabbed him? He was close enough now. She could feel the warmth of his breath against her forehead. He was only inches from her in the darkness.

The men she'd known—all of them—had wanted something when they got this close. And he was big enough to overpower her.

She felt him shift beside her. Then fabric rustling.

"Here, wrap this around you."

Something heavy settled over her shoulders. It took her three sluggish heartbeats to recognize it.

His coat, the leather still warm from his body.

Belle couldn't help but burrow into it, seeking that warmth even as her mind screamed warnings.

"What about you?" The words escaped before she could stop them, her voice barely above a whisper.

Silence answered her from the darkness.

They were both sitting now, leaning against the wall. Coop had settled beside her rather than looming over her. The consideration in that simple action made something in her chest twist.

Belle tried to stay awake, tried to maintain her vigilance, but exhaustion tugged her into sleep again. Her eyelids grew heavy. Her head drooped. She jerked upright.

Drowsed again. Found herself leaning against Coop's shoulder.

His arm came around her. She was too tired to fight it, too cold to push away the warmth he offered. Her body soaked in the heat of his solid presence beside her, and she fell asleep.

Sometime later, she woke with a start, her heart hammering. How much time had passed? Everything but her face was warm. It took her a moment to understand that Coop had folded her into his embrace as they slept. There was nothing inappropriate about it—his hands rested carefully on her shoulders, his breaths even, sharing the heat that had kept them both from freezing in the night.

He was closer than Belle had let anyone get since she'd left the brothel. She could feel the steady rise and fall of his chest against her side, could hear his heartbeat. His hand smoothed down her back in what might have been an unconscious gesture. Every muscle in Belle's body went rigid.

His breathing changed. He was waking up. She felt him come to awareness, and go still. Had he realized how close they were?

The moment stretched between them, tension building. Where was her knife?

Coop's breathing hitched. He was completely awake now.

"I'm not going to hurt you." His voice was rough with sleep.

His hands moved away from her immediately, as if afraid any sudden movement would spook her. He sat back.

Belle found the knife in her lap as she scrambled backward a few inches, shoving his coat back at him. It was slightly warmer now than it had been in the deepest cold of night.

He didn't pursue her. That made her brave enough to ask, "Do you think it's morning?"

A quiet sigh came from the darkness. Was he irritated by her question?

"What if they aren't looking for us?" The fear that had been building in her chest finally found voice.

"They are," Coop said with certainty.

"No one really wants me on the wagon train." The truth finally said out loud.

"That's not true."

Belle couldn't quite read his voice, couldn't tell if he was lying to make her feel better or if he actually believed what he was saying. She was shaking again, but this time it wasn't from the cold. What if they died down here?

"We should keep going. One of these tunnels has to lead outside." She started to stand up.

His hand brushed her shoulder and she jumped, stepped back so quickly that her elbow knocked against the rocky wall.

"You're still scared of me?"

She couldn't answer.

There was a long moment of silence before he spoke.

"Here." He grasped her wrist and pressed something into her hand.

Heavy, cold metal.

Belle's breath caught. "Your gun?"

"I don't want you to be scared of me. Use it on me if you need to."

He was speaking foolishness. Shoot him? Was this a trick?

Belle stood frozen in shock, the weight of the revolver unfamiliar in her hand. No man she'd ever known had done something like this.

She didn't know what it meant. Didn't understand.

"We should keep going," Coop said quietly. "If you can stand it. If we can find a dry piece of wood, maybe I can get enough spark that we could have some light."

She heard him moving, putting his coat back on. The leather creaked softly in the darkness.

"Why don't you hold on to the back of my coat?" he suggested. "So we don't get separated."

For a long moment, Belle didn't move. Holding onto him

meant being close, meant trusting him not to turn on her in the darkness.

But she had a gun in her hand. And the alternative was staying here alone, or losing him in the pitch black of these caves.

Slowly, Belle reached out until her fingers encountered the leather of his coat. She gripped it tightly, the gun still held in her other hand, and allowed herself to be led deeper into the darkness.

Fifteen

ROB ROUSED SLOWLY, his eyes adjusting to the faint light of early morning. The sky was just beginning to brighten along the eastern horizon, but the sun hadn't yet crested the mountains. Earlier than he'd thought, then.

The events of the previous night came rushing back—gunshots echoing through the fog, the chaos, Alice's brothers gone missing. Alice asking him to stay.

No one had really gone to bed in their tents or wagons. Worry had kept them all awake, some of the men still out searching even now.

Rob remained where he'd fallen asleep last night, sprawled on the cold ground near the fire. But he wasn't alone. Alice was tucked into his side, a quilt wrapped around both of their shoulders. His arm was draped over her, and her head rested in that space between his jaw and shoulder that seemed made for her.

Someone had stoked the fire, and it was throwing warmth.

Across from where Alice was curled into Rob, Felicity and Ben were sleeping, the girl pressed against Felicity's side. Maddie sat with her back against a wagon wheel, Alex and Paul tucked under each arm, all three of them dozing. The baby must have been taken to bed sometime in the night.

Rob realized that motion across the campfire had woken him. Collin was moving around quietly, adding wood to the fire, setting a pot of water on to boil for coffee. His movements were quiet, trying not to wake the others though he moved with a stiffness in his shoulder.

Rob closed his eyes for just a moment, letting himself imagine a different life. One where it was his job to protect Alice from even the smallest hurts. One where waking up with her in his arms was ordinary rather than a gift.

He knew the only reason she'd turned to him yesterday was for comfort. But hearing her tell off his grandfather—hearing her declare that accepting any proposal would be her choice alone—had given him a glimmer of hope that he might still win her.

Rob opened his eyes again. The sky continued to grow lighter, soft pink and gold painting the clouds. He began to gently extricate himself from Alice. She murmured something in her sleep, and he froze, but she only burrowed deeper into the quilt and settled again.

He hobbled a few feet away, his leg stiff and aching from being stretched out uncomfortably on the cold ground all night. He didn't care about the discomfort. Being close to Alice had been worth every twinge of pain.

Collin looked up as Rob approached, his expression grim.

He poured coffee into a tin cup and handed it to Rob without a word.

"Has anyone been found?" Rob asked quietly.

Collin shook his head. His gaze flicked over to where Rob had been tucked up with Alice, and something in his expression softened slightly. "You're good for her," he said, so quietly Rob almost missed it.

Rob sipped his coffee, letting the moment—the warmth of the liquid, the welcome in Collin's words, the pride that swelled in his chest—soak in. Over the past week, Alice's brothers had been slowly letting him into their circle. He thought back to the small gestures: Collin asking for his advice on how to handle a wagon repair, Leo including him in a conversation about what they'd do once they reached the Willamette Valley, Owen nodding respectfully when Rob had turned over baby Molly after the dance.

These acts of acceptance had changed how Rob felt about his place here. He was no longer just the wealthy outsider following the company west. He was becoming part of something bigger than himself.

The fog had cleared overnight, and the growing dawn light revealed the landscape. Rob turned to go to his own wagon. Before he took one step, he saw his grandfather standing a dozen yards away, watching him. The old man's expression was unreadable.

"Let me know what you need," Rob said to Collin, then hobbled on his crutch toward his grandfather.

"Come to Oregon with me." The words burst out before Rob could think them through. "I've got plans drawn up for a sawmill. I'm going to make a fortune cutting logs, maybe even add capacity to mill grain in a year or two."

He stopped himself before adding, *We can do it together.*

That would be giving Grandfather control again. Rob didn't need his grandfather's expertise or his money. What he needed was...

What? His approval? His blessing?

No. That wasn't it.

For a moment, Rob thought he saw calculation in his grandfather's eyes. The old man sizing up whether this venture was worth his time. Whether Rob was still controllable.

And Rob realized: he didn't need Grandfather to come. He'd offered out of some desperate, childish hope that maybe they could build something different than what they'd had back East.

But Grandfather would never change. And Rob was done trying to prove himself to a man who only saw him as a legacy to control.

His grandfather's expression hardened. He shook his head, his mouth turning down beneath his silver mustache. "I've got responsibilities back home. Seems you've forgotten yours."

One of the foremen from the mill—a man named Garrett who'd traveled west with Grandfather—stood off to the side, close enough to act as a bodyguard. His presence made this conversation feel even more formal, more final.

Grandfather's voice hardened further. "If you don't come back home, you aren't my grandson anymore. You'll be left out of the will. You'll be as good as dead to me. You've got until tomorrow to decide."

The words hit Rob like a physical blow, stealing the

breath from his lungs. He stood there, stunned, as his grandfather turned on his heel and walked away without another word.

Garrett shifted awkwardly, clearly uncomfortable at having been privy to this conversation. Rob raised his free hand and rubbed the back of his neck, shame flaring.

He'd never imagined that making this choice would mean losing connection with his grandfather altogether. The man who'd raised him, taught him everything about business, been his only family after his parents died. Rob had thought that after he got settled in the West, they could exchange letters. Keep in touch.

Now, even as the grief settled into his chest, Rob shoved the thought aside. Alice needed him. Her brothers were still missing. And he remembered Alice's question from days ago. Could Coop be innocent?

He turned to Garrett. "Who ran the investigation into the explosion?"

The foreman's eyes widened slightly. He glanced in the direction Grandfather had gone, then back to Rob. "Mr. Braddock—"

"I'm asking you, Garrett." Rob kept his voice level. "Not as the mill owner's grandson. As someone who wants to know the truth."

Garrett's jaw worked for a moment. "Your grandfather wouldn't like me to talk about that."

If Coop wasn't involved, he deserved to know. Maybe it would make things easier between him and Leo.

Garrett looked torn, his gaze darting between Rob and the direction Grandfather had gone. He shook his head. "I can't."

He walked away, leaving Rob standing alone with his thoughts.

Rob realized with startling clarity how much he'd changed. A few months ago, he would have accepted Grandfather's orders without question. Would have believed Coop was guilty because it was convenient, because Coop fit the profile of someone who would make that kind of mistake.

But being with Alice had shown him that family still loved you even when things were difficult, even when you made wrong choices. Her brothers might fight with each other, might say harsh words in the heat of anger, but they never stopped being family.

That wasn't something he'd ever experienced with his grandfather. Love, in the Braddock household, had always been conditional—contingent on meeting expectations, on living up to the family name, on doing what was required.

Rob didn't want Coop to be blamed for something he might not have done. For Alice's sake, he hoped her brother was innocent. But even if Coop had made mistakes, even if he'd been drinking that night, Rob understood now that people were more than their worst moments.

Shouts erupted from somewhere beyond the wagons. "We found them! They're alive!"

Rob's heart leaped. He hurried as fast as his injured leg would allow back toward the fire, his crutch sinking into the damp ground with each step.

Alice was sitting up, the quilt pooled around her waist, her hair mussed from sleep. When she saw him approaching, her eyes lit with a warmth that made his chest tighten. Maybe even happiness to see him.

She stood and brushed off her skirts, waited for him. They walked together behind the rush of people heading toward the commotion, Alice matching his slower pace due to his injury.

Several men stood surrounding two figures—Coop and Belle, both of them dirty and exhausted but alive.

Alice gave a little gasp. "Where's August?"

* * *

A day and a half later, Alice walked alongside Felicity, the two women moving with a quiet determination that had become more desperate with each passing hour. The day had been long, filled with the relentless search for August. After finding Belle and Coop yesterday, the group realized the terrain was riddled with dangers—small caves that dropped away into darkness, hidden beneath innocent-looking ground. Caves that could swallow a man whole.

Evening was approaching now, and the shadows stretched longer across the barren landscape. The volcanic rock caught the fading light, turning the jagged formations into strange, otherworldly shapes.

Whoever had shot at Collin hadn't been found. Belle had barely come out of the wagon.

Alice couldn't keep from scanning the tree-line for danger. Leo had urged Felicity and Alice to stay in camp. Felicity had snapped at him. She'd grabbed up August's rifle and marched out of the circled wagons. There had been no talking her out of it. And Alice couldn't let her go alone.

Felicity had grown quieter as the hours passed. Alice watched from the corner of her eye, noting the way her friend's usual warmth had faded into a somber stillness. There were dark circles beneath her eyes that spoke of two sleepless nights.

Alice's mind drifted back to earlier in the day, when she'd been serving coffee to some of the men. She'd overheard Hollis speaking in a low, heavy voice to Leo.

"The wilderness is a big place."

The words had lingered in her thoughts all afternoon. She'd realized then that Hollis was grieving—August was one of his closest friends on the wagon train. The weight of his absence pressed down on everyone, but Hollis and Felicity more than anyone else. Except for Ben, who'd been inconsolable.

"Is Ben all right?" Alice asked gently, breaking the silence between them.

When Felicity spoke, her voice was tight. "Ben's taking it really hard. She blames herself for running off in the fog. It's like August just disappeared."

The guilt in Felicity's own voice was unmistakable. Alice understood it—that terrible weight of wondering if you could have done something different. Why hadn't Alice thought to check on August? He'd hated her coddling and she'd let his words hurt her feelings. She should've done something differently.

The two women had ventured far from camp by now. This area was even more sparse than where they'd camped, with few trees or vegetation to break up the open expanse. The ground was rocky, covered in dark volcanic stone that crunched beneath their feet. Here and there, twisted formations of lava rock jutted up like the bones of some fanciful creature.

"Do you think August could have even come this far?" Felicity's voice broke the silence, barely above a whisper.

"I don't know." Alice's own hope was flagging, worn down by two days of fruitless searching. "But we can't give up."

The one steady presence in Alice's life over the past couple of days had been Rob. Despite the obvious pain from his broken leg, despite having to use that crutch for every movement, he'd stepped in to help wherever he was needed. He'd assisted with food preparation—making those biscuits that had been such a mess at first. He'd kept the children occupied with games and stories, giving the searching adults one less thing to worry about. And he'd been a quiet source of support for Alice, there when she needed a shoulder to lean on, when the panic threatened to overwhelm her.

Alice thought about Rob now, back at camp, with his grandfather still pressuring him to leave. The idea made her chest tighten, so she forced herself to focus on the present. On finding August.

A faint noise caught her attention, the hair on the back of her neck standing up.

They had reached the edge of a wooded area that sloped down the side of the mountain—one of the few places where scraggly trees had managed to take root among the rock. Alice stopped Felicity with a hand on her arm, squinting into the darkening trees.

The feeling of being watched sent a shiver down her spine.

Another sound echoed nearby, this one closer.

Felicity gasped softly. "Did you hear that?"

Alice's eyes swept the terrain, and that's when she noticed it—an open hole in the ground, several feet away, barely visible in the fading light. The shadows and dark rock around it made it blend into the landscape.

"August!" Alice called out, her voice carrying into the darkness below.

"August, are you there?" Felicity's voice joined hers, desperate and pleading.

A faint reply reached them, weak and distant. So faint that Alice couldn't make out the words, only knew it was a human voice.

"He's down there!" Felicity started forward, but Alice caught her arm.

As they crept closer, Alice realized the ground dropped off sharply nearby. What had seemed like flat terrain gave way to a steep decline. One wrong step and they might tumble down after him.

Both women squatted beside the depression.

"August! Can you hear us?" Felicity's voice echoed down into the depths.

His reply was barely audible. Alice couldn't tell if it was from lack of food and water or simply the depth of his fall. How deep was the hole?

"August, we're here!" Alice called, keeping her voice steady despite the fear gnawing at her insides. She spoke to Felicity this time. "I'm going to get help."

"What time of day is it?" August's voice drifted up, strained and confused.

"It's almost dark," Felicity answered, tears on her cheeks.

When August spoke again, his words sent ice through Alice's veins. "There's a cougar. It's been hunting me. Trying to find out if I'll come out of this hole. You need to get to safety."

A cougar. It must have been hunting the wagon train.

Alice and Felicity exchanged a look in the fading light. Felicity clutched the rifle in front of her as Alice's gaze skittered to the tree-line. There was no movement. Nothing out there.

"I'm not leaving him." Felicity's voice was steady now. The defeat from moments ago had been replaced by fierce protectiveness.

"I should have realized it sooner," August's shout was more firm. "Go back to camp!"

"I'll run," Alice said. "Bring help."

Felicity nodded gravely.

Pushing to her feet, aware of the darkness closing in around them, Alice started to run, her feet finding purchase on the rocky ground even as the light disappeared around her. Fear pushed her faster. Worry for August, stuck in that cave as he'd been for days without food or water. Worry for Felicity, vulnerable out in the open.

A distant scream pierced the air—not human, but something wild and predatory. Every hair on Alice's body rose, primal fear clawing at her chest.

The cougar.

She stumbled. Caught sight of the white-covered wagons.

"Help! Leo! Owen!" Her shout was breathless. Could they even hear her?

Just as another scream echoed through the night, a gunshot cracked through the stillness, the sound reverberating off the rocky terrain.

Felicity!

Sixteen

"WHAT ARE YOU DOING OUT HERE?"

Alice looked up from her step in the flickering torchlight. Rob stood leaning on his crutch in the dark, his expression disapproving.

She'd been so focused on not tripping over the treacherous rock that she hadn't realized she and Ben had reached their destination. Alice's arms were full, a blanket draped over one shoulder, a pail of water threatening to slosh over with each step, the dipper clanking against the metal sides. Not far behind her, Ben carried a plate wrapped in cloth, steam still rising from the food hidden beneath.

Alice looked around, taking in what the men had accomplished in the hour since she'd run back to camp with news of August and Felicity's location. Her gaze rested on Felicity and a beat of relief pounded through her. Owen and the others had raced out to the cave after the gunshot. Gerry Bones had come back to camp at a run with news of his own: Felicity had scared away the cougar when it had charged out of the woods at her. Now Felicity's face was pale but determined as she made her way to meet Alice and her adopted daughter.

The men had set up Rob's wagon on the only flat space near the cliff's edge, backing it carefully into position. A long beam had been secured across the wagon bed, and from it hung a pulley system with rope disappearing down into the dark maw of August's cave. The wagon wheels had been chocked with large rocks on all sides—insurance against the vehicle rolling forward over that terrible drop-off. The oxen were still hitched in their traces, their large bodies shifting uneasily in the flickering light.

Torches had been planted in a circle around the rescue site, their flames casting long, dancing shadows across the landscape. A couple of men from the company stood at the edges of the torchlight, rifles in hand, their only job to watch the darkness beyond for any sign of threat.

Owen approached, his expression tight with worry and frustration. "You shouldn't be out here," he said to Alice. "When August gets hauled up out of that hole, he's going to be angry that you've put yourself in danger."

Ben's face was buried in Felicity's skirts, her small frame trembling. But Felicity raised her chin, and Alice saw the steel in her friend's eyes.

"That cougar didn't scare me off," Felicity said firmly. "And you won't either. I aim to see my husband taken care of."

"He's been down there for almost three days with no food or water," Alice added, her arm with Felicity's. "He'll need help the moment he gets out of there."

When she looked back at Rob behind Owen, the warmth

in his eyes made her breath catch, despite everything happening around them.

"I'll keep an eye on them," Rob said to Owen, shifting his weight on his crutch.

Owen returned to where Leo, Collin, and Hollis stood near the rope. They hadn't dared bring more men, not with Sarge out there somewhere and a cougar on the loose. Except for Gerry, the cowboys were with the cattle, and everyone back in the circle of wagons was on high alert.

Rob shifted toward them. "You all right?" he asked Felicity.

"I am. The cat was—frightening. Something about it was…" She shook her head.

"Somethin' was what?" Ben prompted.

"Its gait was off. Maybe it had an injured foot or something."

"Perhaps that's why it charged you?" Alice wondered. "It wanted easy prey?"

"And didn't find any," Rob added.

Alice moved closer to Rob, careful with her burden of supplies. "Thank you for this," she said quietly. "For thinking so quickly."

It had been Rob's idea to use the pulley system from his sawmill supplies, Rob who'd offered his wagon without hesitation when the men were trying to figure out how to safely extract August from a hole too deep to climb down.

"Family is important," Rob said, and the intensity of his gaze that spoke of more than just this rescue.

She felt it. He felt it too.

But now was not the time to dwell on the intangible thing growing between them.

"He's tugged twice!" Leo's voice called out. "That means he's secured himself with the rope. Let's haul him up."

The men began pulling, their movements synchronized. The pulley creaked with the weight, and Alice held her breath.

Rob took a few hobbling steps toward the men. "Slower," he called out. "If he's injured, you might hurt him worse. And you don't know if there are jagged rocks lining the walls of that cave."

The men adjusted their pace, pulling more carefully now. Alice watched with her heart in her throat, a silent prayer moving through her mind over and over. *Please, God. Please let him be all right.*

Felicity's hand found hers, gripping tight. Neither of them spoke.

Owen leaned over the edge of the hole, one hand on the rope. "I can see him!"

But at that moment, a shadow darted out of the woods.

Alice saw it first—a large, low shape moving with frightening speed despite its uneven gait. "Look out!" she shouted.

Before the words left her mouth, a rifle cracked from the other side of the circle of torchlight, the sound deafening in the night air. The wagon creaked ominously as the oxen shifted in their traces.

Alice was suddenly, terrifyingly aware of that dark chasm on the other side of the wagon, where the ground dropped away completely, falling into blackness.

Shouts erupted from the men. The cougar ran toward the oxen, its injured leg not slowing it down as much as Alice had hoped.

Another shot rang out.

The oxen bellowed in fear, trying to get away from the predator. They jerked hard in their traces. Alice watched in horror as one of the rocks chocking the wagon wheels dislodged.

The wagon shifted. Started to rock.

"No!" someone shouted.

Felicity gasped, her hand crushing Alice's. "August—"

Everything was happening too fast. Alice felt frozen, her body locked in place even as her mind screamed at her to move, to do something.

Rob dropped his crutch and hobbled toward the chaos unfolding, his injured leg dragging. He was moving between the men and the wagon when the cougar let out a sound that turned Alice's blood to ice—a low, guttural growl that spoke of hunger and desperation.

The oxen lost all control. They jerked forward with panic-fueled strength. The wagon lurched into motion just as August's head and shoulders appeared over the edge of the cave opening.

The wagon teetered precariously on the edge of the cliff-side, the chasm yawning behind it.

"Stop!" Alice cried, but her voice was lost in the chaos.

* * *

Everything slowed, even Rob's heartbeat.

He saw the flash of tawny fur first, caught in the torchlight as the cougar darted from the scraggly trees. The animal was large, one of its front legs not touching the ground, giving it a lurching, uneven gait.

The oxen bellowed, their massive heads tossing. His wagon rocked forward despite the chunks of rock wedged beneath its wheels.

Rob's heart slammed against his ribs.

August emerged from the dark maw of the cave at that very moment, the rope tied under his arms. Rob could see the top of his head, his shoulders just clearing the edge of the opening. Alice was somewhere behind him.

A rifle cracked. The sound was deafening in the night, echoing off the barren landscape. Another shot followed. The oxen jerked hard in their traces, wild with panic. One of the chocking stones dislodged, rolling away into the darkness with a hollow clatter against the rock.

The wagon lurched forward.

"No!" someone shouted.

The cat ran off into the darkness.

Rob didn't think. His body moved on pure instinct, the same instinct that had made him throw himself between a bullet and Coop Spencer weeks ago. He dropped his crutch, barely registering as it hit the ground.

The wagon was tipping. He could see it happening—the way the back end lifted slightly, the terrible moment where the weight shifted toward the cliff's edge.

If the wagon went over, August would go with it.

Alice would never survive the loss.

Rob threw himself forward. Pain exploded through his broken leg with his first step. White-hot fire shot from his shin to his hip. He felt something shift in the splint, felt the bone grind. His vision blurred for half a second.

He kept moving.

His gait was more lurch than run, his weight pitched forward at a reckless angle. His right leg—the broken one—dragged behind him. Each impact sent fresh agony lancing through him.

The rope. He needed to reach the rope.

The big beam secured across his wagon bed held the pulley system. Ropes stretched from it down to where August hung suspended in the mouth of the cave. Rob's fingers reached for it, his body lurching forward in a desperate dive.

His hand closed over rough hemp.

"Stay back!" he shouted to the women.

He grabbed on with both hands, his weight suddenly supported by his grip alone. For one terrible moment, his feet left the ground entirely as momentum carried him forward. Then his boots hit rock again and he stumbled, nearly going down.

The wagon creaked ominously, shifting closer to the edge.

Rob's mind raced even as his body moved. If the wagon went over the cliff, August would be dragged down with it. The knot securing him to the rope was tied under his arms. Rob had to untie it before—

Rob's right hand flew to the knife strapped to his belt. His fingers fumbled with the leather strap holding it in place.

"Hold the wagon!" He shouted the desperate words even as he worked to free the knife.

Collin and one of the other men had grabbed other ropes tied to the wagon frame, their faces red with strain as they leaned back, trying to slow the inevitable slide toward the cliff. Hollis ran to the oxen, giving the command to pull.

Everything he owned was in that wagon. His sawmill

equipment, his supplies, his tools. His future. The inheritance he'd fought for.

Rob could see it in the men's faces—they weren't strong enough. Not for this. Not against the combined weight of a fully loaded wagon and panicked oxen.

Hollis began sawing at the leather traces, trying to free the animals from the harness before they pulled the wagon over with them.

Rob's knife came free.

The wagon lurched again.

"Untie August!" someone yelled. "The knot's too tight!"

"He's being dragged!"

Rob looked over his shoulder. August's head and shoulders were fully out of the hole now. He was being dragged across the ground, inch by inch.

The oxen broke loose. Hollis had finally succeeded in cutting through the harness. The massive animals crashed away into the darkness.

Without the oxen's weight to anchor it, the wagon tipped further.

There was no choice. Rob used the knife as a saw, but the rope was thick and he was dragged forward. His boots caught on a depression and he lost his balance.

He went down hard, his hip slamming into the ground with bruising force. The impact jolted his broken leg and he cried out.

His fingers were still locked around the rope, but now he was being pulled toward the cliff edge.

No.

Rob sawed harder, his arms burning with the effort of

hanging on, his whole body braced against the terrible pull dragging him closer to the edge.

The wagon groaned as it shifted. Men shouted, their voices overlapping, urgent and frightened. Someone screamed August's name.

The rope began to fray.

Rob's broken leg was screaming. He could feel something wet soaking through the bandages beneath the splint. Blood? Had he reopened the wound? It didn't matter. Nothing mattered except—

The rope snapped.

The recoil sent Rob sprawling backward. He hit the ground hard, the back of his head cracking against the ground. Stars exploded across his vision. Pain radiated from his leg.

There was an awful noise of wood splintering, metal screeching, the hollow thunder of something massive falling with a crash.

Rob forced his eyes open. The world spun sickeningly. He was flat on his back, staring up at a sky full of stars that wheeled overhead like they were dancing. He forced his eyes to focus. Forced his head to turn.

His wagon was gone.

The space where it had been was just... empty. The torches still burned in their circle, casting flickering light across the barren ground. But the wagon had disappeared into the darkness.

Rob tried to take a breath. Everything hurt.

He became aware of footsteps running toward him. Someone was saying his name, but the voice sounded like it was coming from underwater, distant and muffled.

"Rob!"

Alice. That was Alice's voice.

The pain in his leg reached a crescendo that made it hard to think, hard to do anything except lie there and try to remember how to breathe.

Alice knelt over him. Then Doc approached.

Rob forced his eyes open. He hadn't realized they'd closed. Had he blacked out?

Alice's face swam into focus above him, her eyes glistening with unshed tears.

"Is August safe?" His words emerged more groan than anything else.

"Yes. You saved him."

Rob closed his eyes and let darkness take him.

Seventeen

DAWN CREPT over the mountains with the kind of cold clarity that made everything sharp-edged and unforgiving. Rob stood on the slope between the drop off and the bottom of the ravine and stared down at the ruins of his life.

He could barely stand. Shouldn't be on his feet.

He'd barely slept last night. Hadn't been able to face Alice, pretended to be asleep when she'd come to him. With each passing hour, the pain in his leg had worsened. Each breath sent fresh agony lancing up from his shin.

Doc had made it abundantly clear that Rob should be lying still. After Leo and Collin had carried him back to camp, Doc had examined Rob's leg by lamplight.

"Small mercy. You didn't break it again." Doc's expression *had been grave. "But if you don't rest, if you keep putting weight on it, it may never heal correctly." He'd paused. "You could end up with a permanent limp. Or worse."*

Those words chased through Rob's mind all night.

When dawn had neared, he'd pulled himself out of Doc's wagon. He had to know. Was there anything that could be salvaged?

That answer held the one thin thread of hope. It had pushed him out here now.

Rob carefully picked his way down the slope. It was slow going on the treacherous terrain. Loose gravel shifted beneath his boots. The path the wagon had carved in its descent was obvious—a scar of displaced stones and crushed vegetation leading down into the ravine.

His leg screamed with every step. More than once, he had to stop and simply breathe through the white-hot pain.

Part of him—some reckless, angry part—almost hoped that cougar would show itself. Let it come. He had his revolver loaded and ready. That animal had cost him.

As he rounded one last outcropping, the wreckage came into view.

It was so much worse than he'd imagined.

The rising sun illuminated every detail. What remained of his wagon was barely recognizable—just a twisted skeleton of broken boards and crushed metal.

When he finally reached the wreckage, he was leaning heavily against his crutch. His vision swam. His leg throbbed with a deep, sickening ache.

Knowing he'd rather sit than fall down, Rob awkwardly lowered himself to sit beside the mess and began pulling aside debris. Bolts of cloth—the fine fabrics he'd brought for Alice—were torn and filthy, streaked with dirt and lamp oil. He tossed them aside.

Beneath the cloth, he found the china tea set.

Smashed to smithereens. Shards of white china glinting in the morning light.

He'd imagined Alice using this set, had pictured her pouring tea in their future home.

He picked up one of the largest shards, weighed it in his hand. Then threw it as hard as he could.

And then kept digging.

Flour covered everything. The barrels had burst on impact, sending white powder cascading across the wreckage. But it wasn't just flour. The gunpowder barrels had been crushed too, their contents mixing with the flour, with spilled molasses and lamp oil and everything else.

Months of supplies. Ingredients to make food, ammunition for hunting. Gone.

But maybe—

Rob's hands shook as he painfully shifted closer, as he moved boards aside. Maybe the saw blades were intact. They were made of strong metal. Without those, there could be no mill. Without the mill, there was no future in Oregon.

Please, God. Please let them be all right.

He found the first blade buried beneath a tangle of rope and a shattered crate. Rob carefully lifted away the debris.

The warped metal twisted at an angle that made Rob's stomach drop. He ran his fingers along the surface and felt where it had cracked, a hairline fracture that would split completely under the force of cutting timber.

No.

Rob's hands fumbled through sawdust as he dug deeper, searching for the second blade.

His fingers closed around cool metal. He pulled the second blade free.

This one was worse than the first. The impact had bent it nearly double, the metal folded back on itself. Even with access to a blacksmith's forge, it was beyond repair.

Rob dropped it and sat back, his injured leg screaming. A wave of devastation crashed over him.

He'd lost everything.

Until last night, he'd started to believe he was winning Alice over. He'd seen it in her eyes when she'd let him hold her, when she'd defended him to his grandfather. He'd felt it in the way her brothers had slowly begun to accept him.

But he'd lost control in the heat of August's rescue. Again.

Footsteps crunched behind him.

Rob didn't turn around. He knew who it would be even before his grandfather's voice cut through the morning air.

"It's time to put this foolishness to an end."

The words were flat, matter-of-fact. No sympathy. No comfort. Just cold assessment of a situation that had gone exactly as his grandfather had predicted.

Rob didn't respond.

His grandfather moved closer. Rob could feel his gaze, heavy with judgment.

"You've had your foolish lark," Grandfather continued. "And look where it has gotten you. You don't even have a wagon to make your way west. If you decide to continue this madness, it will be on the charity of others."

Each word landed like a blow.

"You're a Braddock," his grandfather said. "It's time to come home."

Rob stared at the bent saw blade, at the blood from his cut hand staining the metal. Everything in him wanted to stand up, to rage at his grandfather. To tell him he was wrong.

But he couldn't make himself move.

Not because his grandfather was right—Rob would never give him that satisfaction.

But because the words hit too close to the truth: he'd failed. Lost control of every situation. Watched his carefully laid plans unravel one by one.

The pattern was undeniable. The fight with Coop—lost control. Following him into the wilderness—lost control. The wagon tipping over the cliff—lost control.

He'd thought he could do it all himself. Thought strength meant never needing anyone, never accepting help. Grandfather had taught him that. Control meant power. Vulnerability meant weakness.

And Rob had believed it. Carried that poison with him all the way to this place.

But now, sitting in the ruins of everything he'd built, Rob realized the terrible truth.

He'd become exactly what he'd been trying to escape.

Rage simmered under his skin—not at Grandfather, not at the situation. At himself. For thinking he could outrun what Grandfather had made him. For believing that refusing Grandfather's path was the same as finding his own.

Grandfather's voice droned on, but Rob barely heard it. The old man's words didn't matter anymore.

What mattered was that Rob had a choice to make. He could go back East, accept defeat, let Grandfather control his future. Or depend on others—take charity. Because he couldn't do it alone.

And Alice deserved so much better than what he could offer her now.

He had nothing. No supplies, no equipment, no way to build the mill he'd promised. No future to give her. He couldn't even walk without assistance. What kind of husband would he be, limping around with a crutch? What kind of provider?

His grandfather was still talking.

"... need to make a crossing back over the Rockies as soon as possible. We can start the journey home today. Your cousins will be glad to see you. The mill needs you, Rob. The family needs you."

Rob's throat tightened. The family. The mill. The life he'd walked away from.

"We'll get you the best doctors back East. In a year or two, this will all be behind you. You can take your proper place at the mill, marry someone appropriate, settle into the life you were meant for."

Someone appropriate. Not Alice.

Rob's hands fisted.

The cold sun beat down on his shoulders. His leg throbbed.

He opened his eyes and stared at the wreckage—at everything he'd lost, everything he'd failed to protect.

His grandfather waited for an answer.

What other choice did he have?

* * *

Alice woke with her face pressed into her pillow, the fabric damp beneath her cheek. Her eyes felt swollen, her lids heavy and gritty. She'd been up far too late, tossing and turning in her bedroll while the events of yesterday played over and over in her mind.

Rob cutting the rope. His wagon disappearing into the darkness. The terrible sounds of wood splintering and metal screeching as everything he owned was destroyed.

She'd gone to talk to him last night. It had been after she'd walked with August and Felicity and Ben into camp. Her brother had been tired and pale but whole. Thanks to Rob. By the time she'd helped get the three of them settled, Rob had been asleep in his bedroll by the fire.

Now morning light filtered through the canvas of her tent, painting everything in shades of gold. Alice pushed herself upright, her body protesting. She'd overslept. The sounds of camp breaking up for the day's travel drifted through the thin walls—the clank of cookware, low voices, horses stamping.

She crawled out of her tent, trying to smooth her hair with one hand. Her dress was wrinkled from sleeping in it. She didn't care.

Felicity sat near the small fire, cradling a tin cup in both hands. When she saw Alice, she lifted one finger to her lips and gestured toward the wagon where August still slept. Felicity's face was drawn with exhaustion, and tension. August was safe, but clearly they hadn't really talked.

Alice moved past her quietly, scanning the camp for Rob.

He was nowhere to be seen.

Her chest tightened. Where would he have gone? Surely Doc wouldn't have let him go far, not with his leg in such terrible condition. She'd seen the way he'd been dragged across the ground last night, heard him cry out in pain.

Movement near the horses caught her attention. Leo was saddling his mount, his movements sharp and abrupt. Each buckle fastened with too much force. Each strap yanked tight. The set of his shoulders radiated anger, the kind of fury that made the air around him feel charged.

Alice's stomach dropped. Something was wrong.

She crossed the distance between them. "Leo?"

He didn't look at her. Just kept working on the saddle, fingers fumbling with the girth strap.

"Leo, what's happened?"

"Talk to your fool brother," he bit out.

"Which one?" The words came out before she could stop them, but Leo wasn't in the mood for humor.

"Coop." He practically spat the name. "That's who."

Alice's mind tried to keep up. "What did he do now?"

Leo yanked the girth strap so hard his horse sidestepped, ears flicking back. For a moment, she thought he might actually answer. Might tell her what had Coop done to earn this level of fury.

Instead, Leo swung himself into the saddle with none of his usual grace. The movement was violent, barely controlled.

"Leo, please—"

"Just stay out of it, Alice." His voice was flat, final. He wheeled his horse around and rode off without another word, leaving her standing alone in the morning chill.

Alice wrapped her arms around herself and watched him disappear into the trees. The familiar ache settled into her chest.

She'd wanted to talk to Leo about Rob. About what the family should do to make things right. But Leo hadn't even paused long enough to hear her. Hadn't asked if she was all right, if she needed anything. Just rode away.

Alice forced herself to move, to start the work that needed doing. But before she could go back to the circle of wagons, she caught sight of Rob leaning on his crutch. But not in camp. Near his grandfather's wagon.

One of his grandfather's men stood close, speaking in low tones. Rob's head was bent, his gaze distant. He seemed upset.

Alice went to him.

"...Spencer..."

She caught her family's name as Garrett spoke to Rob. Was this about Coop? Leo had been riled up. What if it was?

Her stomach pitched.

Garrett noticed her then, his words cutting off mid-sentence.

Rob turned. She barely noticed when Garrett walked away. Rob's face was haggard, lines of pain etched around his mouth and eyes. He looked like he hadn't slept.

"Surely your grandfather can't be worried about Coop out here," she said, the words tumbling out before she'd fully thought them through.

"Not everything is about your brother!" Rob's voice cracked like a whip, so cold that Alice flinched.

She stared at the ground. "I'm sorry."

He didn't look at her.

Something inside her trembled. But she spoke anyway. "Everyone is packing up. The bugle will blow soon. You can ride in—"

"I'm not going." The finality of his words made her stomach knot.

"Rob—"

"My saws are broken." Each word was clipped, controlled in a way that spoke of barely leashed fury. "I have no way to support myself once I reach Oregon. Nothing to trade. I have *nothing*, Alice."

The devastation in his voice struck her like a physical blow. She opened her mouth, the words already forming. *I want to help. Let me help make this right. We can figure this out together.*

"I know you must be—" she started.

"Alice, I'm going home." He cut her off, not even letting her finish the sentence.

He turned away, clearly dismissing her from the conversation. He took a limping step toward his grandfather, who stood yards away.

"I thought you—" *Loved me.* She couldn't say the words, suddenly uncertain.

Rob stopped, his knuckles white where he gripped his crutch. He didn't turn to face her.

The Old Man's gaze skittered over her as if he didn't even see her. There was no acknowledgement. It was like being back in his household all over again.

"You said it yourself," Rob said quietly. "We were never suited."

Alice stood frozen, watching him retreat. The pain in her chest bloomed into something larger, something that threatened to swallow her whole.

A memory crashed over her, sudden and vivid.

Fifteen years old, standing in the tiny kitchen of their tene-

ment. Mama had been dead barely a week. Leo sat at the table, his face hollow with grief, shoulders bowed under the weight of responsibility that had been thrust upon him too young.

"I've been thinking," Alice had started, her voice tentative. "About the household money. If we—"

"Alice." Leo had looked up at her, his eyes flat and exhausted. "I don't need anything except for you to get dinner on the table."

The dismissal had been complete. Absolute. As if her thoughts on their dire financial situation didn't matter. She was only valuable for what she could do.

She'd swallowed her words and her tears and started peeling potatoes.

The memory faded as tears welled in her eyes, hot and sudden.

Her throat closed up, making it hard to breathe. She pressed one hand to her chest, feeling her heart hammer against her ribs with sharp, painful beats.

She'd fallen in love with him.

The realization hit with the force of a physical blow, stealing what little breath she had left. She'd tried so hard not to. Had built walls, kept her distance, reminded herself over and over that Rob Braddock wasn't for her. That they came from different worlds, that her brothers would never accept him, that loving him would only lead to heartbreak.

But somewhere between watching him make those terrible biscuits and listening to him talk about building a mill, between seeing him comfort baby Molly and witnessing him sacrifice everything to save August—somewhere in all of that, her heart had betrayed her.

And he didn't care enough to even listen.

She'd thought he was different. Thought he saw her, really saw her, in a way no one else ever had. He'd held her when she cried. He'd asked about her dreams, her fears. He'd made her feel like she mattered.

Then he'd just... dismissed her. Shut her out. Treated her like she was in the way.

Alice turned and stumbled back toward her tent, toward the familiar work of breaking camp and preparing for another day's travel.

Her emotions didn't matter. She'd learned this lesson before. Why had she let herself forget?

Eighteen

"YOU SEEM UPSET."

The words pulled Alice back to herself, dragging her out of the spiral of thoughts that had been consuming her for hours. She blinked, suddenly aware of her surroundings—the ground beneath her boots, the rhythmic creak of wagon wheels, the bright midmorning sun beating down on her shoulders.

She'd been walking alongside the wagon for awhile without really seeing anything.

August had come alongside her, his expression concerned. Ben clung to her father's hand with both of hers, small fingers wrapped tight around August's larger ones. The little girl hadn't left his side all morning.

August looked pale, his face drawn with exhaustion. But he was upright, walking steadily beside the wagon. Alive. Safe.

Alice tried to make her voice even. "I'm fine." Not true.

August's mouth quirked slightly, and she realized he could

probably hear the falseness in her voice. Of course he could. He'd always been observant.

She tried to change the subject, forcing brightness into her words. "Are you alright? You should probably be resting. Doc said—"

"I've been a fool all these weeks." August's quiet words cut through her deflection. He stopped walking, and Alice stopped too, even though the wagon kept rolling. "I thought... I thought people couldn't need me anymore. Not the way I am now."

Alice's throat tightened. "That's foolish talk."

"I know." A rueful smile touched his lips. "I had a lot of time to think down there in that hole."

"That's not funny, August."

"Hush, now. Let me finish." His hand waved between them. "One of the things I realized is how badly I've treated you. You, specifically, Alice."

Alice's throat went tight. "You don't have to—"

"I do." August's voice was firm. "You tried to help me. More than once. And I pushed you away. Told you to leave off." He shook his head, his expression pained. "I saw you as one more reminder of what I'd lost. Every time you offered help, it felt like you were saying I couldn't do it myself. That I wasn't capable anymore.

"But you weren't saying that at all, were you?" August continued. "You were just being you. Trying to help someone you care about adjust to something impossible. And I pushed you away.

"I'm sorry, Alice. I'm so sorry for pushing you away when you were only trying to love me like family should."

A tear slipped down Alice's cheek. She'd needed to hear this more than she'd realized.

Ben tugged on his hand, and they started forward again. The girl tipped her head back to the sky, singing to herself. Not paying attention to the adults beside her.

August was quiet for a long moment "What's got you upset? Is it Coop? Or Rob?"

Alice's steps faltered. She'd hoped he would forget what he'd asked her. "Neither. Both. Maybe."

The words tangled in her throat. He didn't push. Maybe that's what made it easier to keep going.

"I thought..." She stopped, started again. "I thought I was falling in love with Rob. But he doesn't want me anymore." That wasn't quite right. Something about the statement niggled at her.

August waited.

"The Old Man treated me—treated all the servants—like we were invisible. That's part of why I pushed Rob away for so long." She hadn't meant to fall for him. Or to believe someone like him could love her. "I should've known better. I'm used to being overlooked. It shouldn't hurt—"

"What's this foolishness?" August's voice sharpened slightly.

"Leo. Coop. Rob. God." The admission came out small. "I prayed so hard for Mama to get better, and God didn't see me. He didn't answer."

The sun was warm. Around them, the wagon train moved steadily forward. But Alice felt frozen, trapped in a moment from years ago when she'd knelt beside her mother's sickbed and begged God for a miracle that never came.

"Alice." August's voice was gentle but firm. "Do you know the story of Hagar?"

She blinked at the seemingly random question. "From the Bible?"

"She was a slave. Cast out by her masters with nothing—no food, no water, no hope. Left to die in the desert with her son."

Alice remembered the story but it had been a long time since she'd read from the family Bible.

August seemed to listen for a moment, head tipped toward Ben, who was now humming, still holding his hand. He seemed satisfied that she wasn't paying attention.

"She thought she was going to watch her child die," August said quietly. "She couldn't bear it, so she put him under a bush and walked away so she wouldn't have to see. And that's when God showed up."

The wagon ahead of them hit a rough patch, jostling over a rock. Alice barely noticed.

"God saw her," August said. "A servant woman. A slave. Someone society deemed worthless. And God heard her son's cries. He provided water, saved their lives, and promised that her son would become a great nation."

Alice's eyes smarted with sudden tears.

"God sees you, Alice," August said firmly. "Maybe He didn't give you the answer you asked for, but He's never abandoned you. He's never stopped watching over you. The same way you…" a momentary hesitation, "and Felicity never stopped trying to find me."

The words settled into Alice's chest, warm and heavy. She thought about Felicity's determination. Felicity had never given up on August, even when hope seemed lost.

Had God been doing the same for Alice all this time?

Alice's mind raced backward through the years. After Mama died, when they'd had nothing, God had provided jobs for Leo and for her at the Braddock estate. When they'd needed to flee New Jersey, He'd led them to Hollis's wagon train. When August had been lost, God had guided them to him in that cave.

God had provided friends when she needed them. Maddie and Felicity, Stella and Evangeline. Women who saw her, who valued her, who treated her like she mattered.

He'd kept their family together through impossible circumstances—through Mama's death, through poverty, through Coop's reckless choices and Leo's stubborn pride.

And He'd brought Rob into her life. A man who'd looked at her and seen someone worth crossing a continent for. Someone worth losing everything for.

Alice stopped walking entirely, one hand pressed to her chest where her heart hammered against her ribs.

"I can't base my decision on today," she whispered, the words tumbling out as the truth crystallized. "What Rob showed today... that's not who he's been these past weeks."

August listened. Even Ben perked up at the fervor in Alice's voice.

"He's let his grandfather influence him." Maybe manipulate him in a moment of weakness.

A weight lifted. She turned to August. "I let him walk away."

"Because he pushed you away." Her brother didn't seem willing to let her take all the blame.

Alice looked past him, to where the wagon train stretched

ahead, disappearing over a rise one at a time. She glanced over her shoulder, to the East. Rob was back there somewhere.

"I've made a horrible mistake," Alice whispered. "I have to go to him."

But August's expression shifted to concern. "You can't ride out alone. Between Sarge and that cougar—"

"I'll be all right," she reassured him.

He reached out and grabbed her forearm. "Alice, no."

Her brother was back. Protective streak and all.

Joy filled her at the knowledge that August was more himself than he'd been for weeks.

"I'll be careful," she promised.

He called out after her, but she was already rushing toward Stella's wagon.

She would be quick. Take a rifle. It was daylight and the wagons hadn't traveled that far.

All she could think of was her desperate need to get to Rob.

* * *

"What do you think you're doing?"

Rob didn't move from where he lay in the back of one of his grandfather's wagons, one arm thrown over his face to block out the sun. The voice was familiar—Leo's—but Rob couldn't find the energy to care.

Around him, he could hear his grandfather's men breaking down the last of their camp. The clink of tin plates being stacked. The thud of supplies being loaded into wagons.

Muted conversation he couldn't quite make out and didn't care to decipher.

"I said, what do you think you're doing?" Leo's voice was closer now, sharper.

Rob finally lowered his arm and squinted up. Leo sat astride his horse, looking down from the saddle at Rob lying flat in the wagon bed. Alice's brother was hard to read in the bright sunlight.

Rob let his arm fall back over his face. "Go away."

"That's what I thought." There was a scoffing tone in Leo's voice, as if Rob had confirmed exactly what he'd expected.

Hoofbeats shifted, leather creaked. Leo wasn't leaving.

"What are you doing out here?" Rob finally asked, his voice muffled by his own arm. "Everyone's gone already."

The wagon train had rolled out hours ago. Rob had listened to the last of the wagons as they disappeared over the ridge. Toward a future no longer for him.

"Evangeline asked me to talk to you," Leo said. "But you were nowhere to be found in the company. One of the cowboys told me they'd seen you with your grandfather, so I rode back."

Rob said nothing. What was there to say?

"So you've finally given up your courtship of Alice."

The words hit like a fist to his gut, stealing what little breath he had left. Rob's hand clenched into a fist against his face, his jaw tightening until his teeth ached.

He didn't want to think about Alice. Didn't want to remember the hurt in her eyes this morning when he'd cut her off, dismissed her attempts to help. The way she'd stood there, small and wounded, while he'd turned his back and limped away.

Leo kept on. "You know, it's a good thing you decided to leave. Alice doesn't need someone who will give up when times are hard."

Regret, hot and sharp, twisted in Rob's chest. His arm fell away from his face and he pushed himself upright, ignoring the screaming protest from his broken leg.

"I've lost everything!" The words burst out of him, raw and ragged. "My wagon, my equipment, my sawmill plans, my future—"

"You didn't lose your life," Leo said evenly. "You didn't lose your smarts."

Rob stared at him, breathing hard. Around them, Garrett and the other men were still packing but clearly listening to the exchange. Rob felt the weight of their judgment.

"Easy for you to say." Rob's voice came out bitter. "You didn't just watch months of planning burn to ash."

Leo stared at Rob. "What are you really afraid of?"

Rob's jaw clenched. "I'm not afraid."

"You're terrified." Leo leaned forward in his saddle, his eyes boring into Rob. "Terrified of needing help. Terrified of not being in control."

"I don't need a sermon from you." Rob's voice went hard, defensive. This was too close, too real.

"Then answer me this." Leo's voice dropped, became quieter but somehow more piercing. "Would you let Alice make her own choice? Or do you need to control that, too?"

Rob opened his mouth to argue, then closed it again.

"Because that's what you're doing right now," Leo continued, relentless. "Lying in this wagon, making decisions for her. Deciding that she's better off without you. Deciding that she doesn't get a say in whether or not she wants to help you rebuild."

"She deserves better—"

"She deserves a man who trusts her." Leo's voice cracked like a whip. "Who respects her enough to let her choose. But you can't do that, can you? Because if you let her choose, you might need her. And needing someone means you're not in control."

Rob felt something crack in his chest, like ice breaking under too much pressure. "I can't support her. I have nothing to offer."

"Family takes care of each other," Leo said simply. "That's what Evangeline wanted to talk to you about."

Rob frowned, confused.

"She wants to continue her father's legacy," Leo continued. "But she doesn't have the know-how to run one of his sawmills. She wants you to partner with us."

The words took a moment to register. When they did, Rob felt that defensive wall slam back up.

"Partner." The word came out flat. "You mean charity."

"There it is." Leo's eyes narrowed. "I thought I heard your grandfather's voice. The same pride that's been controlling you this whole time. You'd rather lose Alice than accept help from anyone."

"It's not pride—"

"Then what is it?" Leo demanded. "Because from where I'm sitting, it looks like you're so busy trying to do everything yourself, to prove you can provide and protect and control every outcome, that you can't see what's right in front of you."

Rob's breathing came harsh and fast. His hands were shaking. "You don't understand—"

Leo's voice softened. "Here's the thing, Braddock—being strong doesn't mean doing everything alone. Sometimes the strongest thing you can do is admit you need help."

The words settled into Rob's chest, heavy and undeniable.

Rob thought about Alice's face this morning. The way she'd tried to help him, and he'd pushed her away. Not because she couldn't help. But because accepting her help would mean admitting he needed her. Would mean giving up control.

He thought about his grandfather, standing rigid beside his own wagon, making demands and ultimatums. Always needing to be in control. Always alone.

"I don't want to be like him," Rob said, the words barely audible. "Like my grandfather."

"Then don't be." Leo's expression shifted, became something closer to understanding. "Let people help you. Let Alice love you—really love you, which means letting her see all of it. The broken parts. The parts that need help."

Rob closed his eyes, feeling the truth of it wash over him like cold water. He'd been so terrified of being vulnerable, of being seen as weak, that he'd pushed away the one person who saw him completely.

"What if I fail?" The admission came out raw, vulnerable in a way Rob had never allowed himself to be.

"Then you fail," Leo said simply. "And we pick you back up. That's what family does."

Family. The word echoed in Rob's mind. He'd spent his

whole life believing that love was conditional—that he had to earn it through strength and control and never needing anyone. But Alice's family didn't work that way. They fought and argued and drove each other crazy, but they never stopped being family.

Maybe that was the truth he'd been missing all along. That real strength wasn't about control. It was about trust.

Rob opened his eyes and met Leo's gaze. "I need help."

The words felt like a breaking open. Like shedding armor he'd been wearing for so long he'd forgotten what it felt like to be without it.

Leo nodded slowly. "I know."

"I can't do this alone." Rob's voice grew stronger, more certain. "I need your partnership. I need Alice. I need—" He stopped, forcing himself to say the hardest part. "I need God. I can't control everything, and trying to is just going to leave me alone in the back of this wagon while the world moves on without me."

Leo's expression shifted. Not quite approval, but close.

"So what are you going to do about it?" Leo asked.

Rob looked down at his broken leg. At the physical evidence of his weakness. Then he looked past Leo, toward where the wagon train had disappeared hours ago.

"I'm going to go get her," Rob said. "I'm going to tell her I'm terrified and I don't have it all figured out and I need her help. And I'm going to let her decide if that's enough."

Leo's mouth twitched. Might have been a smile. "That sounds an awful lot like trust."

"Yeah." Rob took a shaky breath. "It does."

He started pushing himself toward the edge of the wagon,

pain shooting through his leg with every movement. But he didn't stop. Couldn't stop. Because for the first time in his life, he was choosing right.

And it felt like freedom.

Garrett called that they were ready to pull out.

Rob gritted his teeth and kept moving, his good leg taking the brunt of his weight as his boot hit the ground.

"What are you doing?" His grandfather's chilly voice cut through the air.

Rob looked up to find the old man approaching the wagon, his expression thunderous.

"I'm going back," Rob said, his voice steady. "I can't walk away from Alice."

His grandfather's expression went cold, every trace of warmth or affection draining from his features. When he spoke, his voice was flat, final.

"Then I disown you. You're not my grandson anymore."

The words should have hurt. Should have felt like a loss.

Instead, Rob felt... free.

He steadied himself, his hand still gripping the wagon. His eyes found Leo's, and something passed between them— understanding, maybe. Acceptance.

Leo dismounted and moved to Rob's side, offering his shoulder for support. Rob accepted it without hesitation, leaning heavily on Leo as they hobbled toward Leo's horse.

"Can you ride?" Leo asked quietly.

"Probably, but Doc'll be angry."

Leo chuckled.

It took both of them and Garrett's reluctant assistance to get Rob into the saddle. His broken leg screamed with every movement, but Rob forced himself through it. Once mounted, he gathered the reins and nodded to Leo.

His grandfather stood rigid beside his wagon, watching with an expression carved from stone. Garrett and the other men had stopped working entirely, all eyes on the scene unfolding before them.

Rob met his grandfather's gaze one last time. No words passed between them. There was nothing left to say.

He was going back.

Nineteen

THEY'D BEEN TRAVELING for close to two hours when Rob first caught sight of the familiar landmarks. The jagged outcropping of rock. The twisted pine trees that marked the spot where everything had gone wrong.

Rob shifted in the saddle, trying to ease the constant throb in his leg. Every step the horse took sent fresh pain radiating, a reminder of how badly he'd damaged the injury yesterday. Doc was going to have his hide when they caught up to the wagon train.

Part of him wished Leo had a horse too, so they could move faster. But Leo walked with steady determination beside him, rifle in hand, his eyes scanning the terrain with the practiced vigilance of someone who'd spent months on the trail.

The other part of Rob was grateful for the slower pace. His leg couldn't take much more jarring.

"How much farther?" Rob asked through gritted teeth.

"Can't be more than another hour or two," Leo said

without breaking stride. "Depending on how fast they've been moving."

Rob let his gaze sweep the landscape ahead. Any movement could mean danger.

Suddenly, he spotted a rider coming toward them. His heart stuttered. His hand dropped instinctively to his rifle in the scabbard of the saddle, then relaxed as the figure drew closer. Even from this distance he could see the way the rider sat the horse. Recognized the determined set of those shoulders.

Alice.

His heart leapt.

She was riding Stella's big black stallion, moving purposefully and quickly.

Then her posture changed. She must've caught sight of him.

His chest expanded with a feeling so fierce and overwhelming it almost hurt. Love. Pure, uncomplicated love for this woman who'd turned around and come back for him, riding toward him with an expression of absolute determination on her beautiful face.

How had he ever walked away from her?

He'd been such a fool this morning.

"Is that—" Leo's words cut off sharply.

Rob's attention snapped back to their surroundings, awareness prickling the hair at his nape.

There. In one of the two tall pines just ahead of where Alice was riding, a flicker of movement.

The shape resolved into a tawny form pressed against the trunk, blending so perfectly with the bark that it was nearly invisible.

The cougar.

Its tail twitched. The only movement. A predator waiting to strike.

"Alice!" Leo shouted.

Rob didn't think. Didn't hesitate. Didn't stop to weigh his options or plan his approach.

He kicked Leo's horse hard, gritting his teeth as the sudden motion sent agony lancing through his broken leg. The horse leaped forward, hooves pounding.

Rob drew his rifle, brought it up one-handed while his other hand gripped the reins. The horse was still surging forward when he fired.

The shot cracked through the air.

Missed.

The cat didn't stop.

The cougar launched itself from the tree branch just as Alice passed beneath, a streak of tawny muscle and claws descending like death from above.

Alice screamed.

She tried to rein in the horse, but the stallion panicked. The cat missed by inches, landed on the ground just behind the horse's hindquarters.

The horse bolted.

Alice fell from the saddle.

Rob was almost there.

The cat crouched, ready to pounce again.

Alice wasn't moving.

No.

Rob threw himself from the horse. His body slammed into

the cougar's shoulder mid-leap, his momentum tumbling them both sideways. They hit the ground hard, the impact driving the air from Rob's lungs. Pain exploded through his leg—white-hot and blinding—but he couldn't stop.

His rifle was gone, knocked from his grip. Claws ripped through his sleeve and shoulder.

Alice. He had to keep the cat away from Alice. But he couldn't get a good hold on it.

The cougar twisted beneath him with terrifying strength, its body all sinew and muscle. Rob caught a flash of yellow eyes, of fangs as the cat's head whipped toward him.

He threw his arm up instinctively. Felt teeth scrape his forearm, the thick wool of his coat saving him from a deeper wound.

Leo shouted. A panicked horse screamed a high-pitched whinny.

The cat's claws found purchase, ripping down Rob's shoulder, through coat and shirt and skin. Rob gritted his teeth but didn't let go. Alice was too close.

He fumbled for the knife at his waist, fingers clumsy with pain and panic, trying to shield his face from those fangs. He pulled the blade free just as the cougar's claws raked across his shoulder again.

Hot blood soaked through his shirt. The cat's weight pressed down on him, crushing, suffocating.

I can't lose control. I can't—

No. That wasn't right.

God's in control.

The truth settled over him. He didn't need to control this situation. He just needed to do what had to be done.

Protect Alice. He would die before he let this animal hurt her.

Rob drove the knife upward, felt it sink into the cat's chest. The cougar went limp at the same moment a deafening gunshot cracked.

Rob lay gasping for air, the dead weight of the animal pressing down on his legs. His vision swam, dark spots dancing at the edges.

"I'm not sure that shot did anything." Leo's voice came from above him, breathless and shaky. "I think you had him anyway."

Leo bent down, grabbed the cougar by its scruff, and hauled it off Rob's legs. The movement sent fresh agony through Rob's broken leg and he couldn't suppress the groan that tore from his throat.

Then Alice was beside him, disheveled and beautiful. On knees beside him, sobbing.

Her arms came around his shoulders—then she jerked back with a gasp, staring at the blood soaking through his sleeve.

"Rob—your shoulder—"

He couldn't stop staring at her beautiful face. She was alive. That was all that mattered.

"Are you injured?" His voice came out rough, barely more than a rasp. "You got thrown."

She shook her head, tears streaming down her cheeks. "Leo! I need bandages! Rob's bleeding—"

"I'm alright," Rob said as he forced himself upright, reaching for her hand. "I'm okay, Alice."

His fingers closed around hers, and he felt her trembling.

Her words came in little hiccupping gasps between sobs. "What about your leg?"

"Doc will probably have my hide for jumping off the horse like that," Rob admitted, managing something that might have been a smile. His shoulder burned like fire and his leg throbbed with a deep ache.

But Alice was safe. That was worth everything.

"I couldn't let that cat hurt you," he said, his grip tightening on her hand.

Her eyes met his, wide and bright with tears, and Rob saw everything he needed to see there. She'd come back. She'd ridden out to find him.

And he was never letting her go again.

* * *

Alice couldn't help herself. The tears came in a rush, hot and overwhelming, spilling down her cheeks before she could stop them.

"Aw, Alice." Leo's voice was gentle from somewhere behind her. "He's alright. He said so, didn't he?"

But she couldn't seem to stop. The terror of watching that cougar leap from the tree, of seeing Rob throw himself at it, of those terrible moments when they'd been tangled together—claws and teeth and blood—it all came crashing down on her at once.

Rob gathered her close, his arms coming around her despite his pain. Alice was careful to keep her weight off his injured leg as she practically climbed into his lap, curling her arms around his neck and pressing her face into the warm space between his shoulder and throat.

They were alive. They were both alive.

His heart beat steady and strong beneath her cheek. His arms tightened around her, holding her as if she were something precious. One of his hands came up to cradle the back of her head, his fingers tangling gently in her hair.

"I'm sorry," he whispered into her hair, his breath warm against her temple. "I'm so sorry for what I said this morning. I didn't mean to hurt you. I should've listened to you."

Alice sniffled, pulling back just enough to see his face. His eyes were shadowed with pain—not just physical, but a deeper pain of regret.

"I was coming after you," she said, her voice thick with tears.

Something fierce and tender blazed in his eyes.

Before he could respond, Leo appeared at Rob's side with a strip of cloth torn from one of his shirts. "Let's get that arm bound up before you bleed all over my sister."

Alice reluctantly pulled away, wiping her face with the back of her hand. Together, she and Leo bandaged the deep gouges on Rob's shoulder where the cougar's claws had torn through. Alice's hands trembled as she helped press the cloth against the cuts.

"Doc better have a look at this when we get back to camp." Leo glanced at Alice, his jaw tightening. "I can't believe Collin let you ride out here on your own."

She hadn't exactly asked.

"She doesn't need anyone's permission." Rob's voice was quiet but firm.

Alice's eyes flew to his face. He was looking at her with such intensity that her breath caught. As if he saw her. Really saw her. The way no one else ever had.

"I was coming back to you, too." Rob's gaze slid to Leo, something passing between the two men. "After your brother set me straight."

Alice's hands stilled on the last knot of the bandage. "What about your grandfather?"

Leo had moved away to check on the horses. His voice carried back to them, matter-of-fact. "Disowned him. Said he might as well be dead to him."

The words hit Alice like a blow. She turned back to Rob, searching his face for the devastation such a rejection should have caused. She could see shadows there, pain in the tightness around his eyes. But there was something else too—something that looked almost like freedom.

"I'm sorry," she whispered, reaching for his hand with both of hers. "That's an awful thing to say to someone."

Rob's fingers curled around hers, his grip warm and steady. "I will always choose you, Alice. You're everything to me."

The words washed over her like sunlight breaking through storm clouds. Joy rose up inside her chest, so fierce and overwhelming that she thought she might burst with it. Love more real than anything she'd ever felt flooded through her veins.

She started to lean in, her eyes already closing in anticipation of his kiss, when Leo's voice rang out.

"I'm gonna go fetch Stella's horse so we can get back to camp!"

Alice pulled back, heat flooding her cheeks. When she

looked at Rob, he had a patient half-smile on his face, his eyes crinkling at the corners with barely suppressed amusement.

"What?" she asked, her own lips twitching.

"Nothing." But his smile deepened, and she felt her heart flip in her chest.

"I'm glad you were coming back," she said, the words tumbling out in a rush. "Because I want you to stay, Rob. Come to Oregon. We are suited, you and I."

She watched joy break quietly over his features. His expression softened, transformed by something so tender it made her throat tighten.

"I'm glad you finally realized it," he said, his voice rough with emotion. "Because I love you, and I never want to be without you another day."

A tear rolled down her cheek—a happy tear this time.

"I love you too," she whispered.

Rob's hand came up to cup her cheek, his thumb brushing away the moisture. His touch was gentle, reverent, as if she were made of something fragile and precious. Then he drew her close and kissed her.

The world narrowed to this single moment. To the warmth of his lips against hers, soft and sure. To the way his hand cradled her face while his other arm came around her waist, drawing her closer. To the feeling of coming home after a long, hard journey.

This was right where she belonged.

Alice's hands slid up to rest against his chest, feeling the steady thrum of his heart beneath her palms. Rob's kiss was tender but thorough, speaking of promises and forever and all the words they hadn't yet found time to say.

When he pulled back slightly, his forehead rested against hers, both of them breathing unsteadily.

She'd spent so long believing she was invisible. Believing that what she wanted didn't matter, that her voice would never be heard. But Rob saw her. He'd always seen her, from that very first moment in the upstairs hallway. And he'd crossed a continent, given up everything, to prove it.

She wasn't invisible. She was loved.

Rob's hand moved to tuck a strand of hair behind her ear, his fingers lingering against her temple. His gaze had dropped, and when he spoke, his voice was quiet, almost uncertain.

"I don't have anything to offer you right now, but when I can put aside a little bit for our future, I will ask you to be my wife."

Silly man. The thought came with such fondness that Alice felt tears prick her eyes again. Didn't he understand yet?

She leaned up and kissed him again, softer this time. Sweeter. A kiss that she hoped conveyed everything she felt—that she didn't need his money or his prospects or anything else. She only needed him. His heart, his strength, his stubbornness. The way he looked at her like she was the most important person in his world.

The only thing she needed was Rob himself.

The sound of hoofbeats approaching broke them apart. Alice pulled back, her cheeks warm, and saw Leo leading Stella's black gelding toward them.

"Come on, you two," Leo called, his tone dry but not unkind. "We've gotta catch up to the company before they get worried about us."

Alice stood carefully, then reached down to help Rob to his feet. She saw pain flash across his face, quickly masked.

He caught her concern and leaned heavily on her.

"I'm okay," he said, but his voice was tight.

She knew he wasn't. Knew it would be a long time before that leg healed properly. But she also knew better than to argue with him about it now.

Leo helped boost him into the saddle and then Alice up behind him. Having her arm around him was a relief.

As they carefully turned the horses westward, Alice settled inside with a sense of rightness. Of peace.

She was ready for their future to begin.

God had seen her all along. Had been writing her story even when she couldn't see His hand at work. Had brought her Rob—a man who loved her not for what she could do for him, but for who she was.

Alice pressed her jaw behind Rob's neck, caught the tender smile he gave her over his shoulder.

Together, they would face whatever came next.

She was ready.

Twenty

THE RHYTHM of the wagon wheels had become as
familiar to August as his own heartbeat. The morning sun
warmed his face. He could hear the wagons creaking and
groaning over the rocky trail, could feel the vibration of their
passage through the ground beneath his boots. Ben walked
beside him, her small hand tucked into the crook of his elbow.
She'd been his constant shadow since Hollis and his men had
pulled August from that cave.

"Ben." He waited until he felt her attention shift to him.
"Do you see Felicity?"

The little girl's grip tightened on his arm, and he felt the
tension in her silence. She'd been clinging to him for two days
now, terrified to let him out of her sight.

And he knew it was his job to fix this. He carefully drew
her away, out of the flow of wagons and other pioneers walking, to the edge of the trail where it was quieter. Knelt so that
he was on her level. She rested one hand on his shoulder.

"I want you to know that what happened to me—falling in that cave—wasn't your fault."

He heard the catch in her breath. Went on, "We've talked, you and me and Felicity, about why we don't want you to run off. There's a lot of dangerous things out here in the wild. People, too. It's important to stay close to our family. It's for your protection."

He sensed the motion of her slow nod.

"I didn't do the very thing I asked you to do. Once I got out of the circle of wagons, got disoriented, I should've stopped walking. Stayed still until someone came for me."

A sniffle from her. "But if I wouldn't a run off looking for Felicity—"

He rested his hand on her small shoulder, shook her slightly to interrupt.

"I knew better," he said firmly. "I let my own pride get me. And I could've died if not for Felicity and Alice looking for me."

The truth of it hit him hard all over again, closing off his breath. He had to clear his throat before he could speak again. "What happened wasn't your fault. It was mine. And I won't do it again."

Her sniffle turned to a soft sob. He caught her with only a minor wobble when she threw herself into his arms. Patted her back until she quieted, her head tucked on his shoulder.

"I don't want ya to get hurt." Her voice quaked.

"I don't want that either, but it isn't a little girl's job to watch over her pa."

She drew a steadying breath. "Maybe I could help? When ya need it?"

He smiled gently. "Of course. I'll need a lot of help. From both you and Felicity."

She was more steady as he straightened, and when she took his hand again, her touch was relaxed. She almost skipped by his side.

It didn't take long to catch up to their wagon. He tried to orient himself by the sounds of footsteps and voices. The Spencer wagon should be just ahead—he could hear Alice's voice, and that would mean Felicity wasn't far.

"Did I hear Paul and Alex not far behind us? Why don't you go play with them for a few minutes?"

She only hesitated for a moment before she said, "All right," in a brave tone. And scampered off.

He walked alone, feeling a faint pride that he'd made things right with one of the most important females in his life. Now to figure out how to say what he needed to say to Felicity.

As he took a step forward, his boot caught on something— a rock, maybe, or an uneven patch of ground—and he stumbled.

Then a hand was there, steadying him. Small fingers wrapped around his forearm, her touch light but sure.

Felicity.

She didn't speak, just held him until he'd regained his footing. Then, as quickly as she'd reached for him, she pulled away.

This was it. The moment he could fix everything. Or suffer the loss of the woman he loved because of his own foolish actions.

"Thank you," he said, his voice rougher than he'd intended. "For finding me. For not giving up hope."

He could almost feel surprise radiating off her in waves.

August reached out, his hand searching the space between them. For a breathless moment, he waited.

Then her hand slipped into his.

Relief flooded through him so powerfully it nearly buckled his knees. He drew her hand through the crook of his elbow, holding it there with his hand covering hers.

"It's been too long since we've walked like this," he said quietly.

She drew in a sharp little breath but still didn't speak. August recognized the silence for what it was—the same careful distance he'd been maintaining for weeks. The wall he'd built between them, brick by painful brick.

"That's my fault," he said, forcing the words past the tightness in his throat. He had to clear it before continuing. "For pushing you away."

The wagon wheels creaked. Somewhere ahead, a child laughed. The world kept moving around them. August felt more exposed than when he'd told her his feelings that first time.

"Alice told me," he continued, "how you never stopped looking for me. After I was foolish enough to walk out of camp and get myself into a deadly situation."

"Of course I didn't stop." Felicity's voice was soft, almost a whisper. "You're my husband."

The words hung between them, weighted.

"I would never give up looking for you."

Give up. The words hit him like a physical blow. Suddenly, he wasn't standing beside the wagon train anymore. He was back in the cave, in the absolute darkness that became his prison.

How long had it been? A day, at least. Maybe longer. He had lost track of time in the blackness, his only measure the periods when exhaustion dragged him into fitful sleep.

His hands were ruined. He could feel this even without seeing—the way his fingers trembled when he tried to flex them, the sticky warmth of blood that had dried and cracked and bled again. He'd spent hours trying to dig through the rockslide that blocked the tunnel, his fingernails breaking, his palms scraping raw against unforgiving stone.

It was useless. The rocks were too large, too tightly wedged. He'd accomplished nothing.

He should give up.

The thought settled into his mind with terrible finality. What was the point? Even if someone found him, even if they somehow got him out of this hole—what then? He was blind. Useless. A burden his family would have to carry for the rest of their lives.

That scream came again—the one he'd been hearing periodically from somewhere above. High-pitched and unnatural, it echoed through the cave system and raised every hair on his body.

August leaned his head back against the cold rock wall and closed his eyes. Not that it made any difference in the absolute darkness.

Maybe it would be better for everyone if he just... stayed here.

A squeeze of Felicity's hand on his arm pulled him back to the present, to sunlight and wagon wheels and the warmth of her hand in his. August's breath shuddered.

"I haven't been the husband I should've been," he said, the words scraping out of him. "I thought when I lost my sight, I lost everything."

Felicity was silent for a long moment. When she spoke, her voice was thick with emotion. "You didn't lose me."

The simple statement nearly undid him. August stopped walking, his hand tightening over hers where it rested in the crook of his arm.

"I can't—" His voice broke. "I don't deserve your forgiveness."

"Maybe you should ask for it."

August swallowed hard. His pride flared but he shoved it away.

"Will you forgive me?" The words came out gravelly, barely more than a whisper. "For pushing you away. For hurting you and saying our marriage was a mistake—"

"Of course I forgive you." She didn't wait for him to finish. "I can't imagine how hard this has been for you, August. I only wish you hadn't been trying to work through it alone."

Alone.

The cave pressed in from all sides, the darkness so complete it felt like a living thing. August's throat was raw from shouting, from calling for help that never came. His water was long gone. The hunger gnawed at his stomach, but worse than that was the thirst.

"Why?" The word echoed off unseen walls. "Why did this happen to me?"

He'd asked the question a hundred times—to God, to the universe, to the darkness itself. Never got an answer.

This wouldn't have happened if he still had his sight. Even in that dense fog, he would have seen the hole. Would have recognized the danger. Would have kept Ben safe. What if she'd fallen somewhere too?

That scream came again—closer this time. And with it, a smell. Rotten. Putrid. The stench of death and decay.

August's every sense went alert.

A low growl rumbled from somewhere above him and understanding crashed over him.

Cougar.

That scream had been a cougar all along. The predator was up there, at the mouth of the cave, waiting. Waiting to see if August would try to climb out. Waiting to attack.

The missing calf from two weeks ago. The chicken that had vanished from the Johnsons' wagon. The dog that had run off and never come back.

If he'd still had his sight, he would have recognized the signs. Would have known a predator was stalking the wagon train. Would have been able to protect them.

But he was blind now. Useless as a scout. Couldn't see tracks, couldn't read signs, couldn't do the one thing he'd always been good at.

What kind of future could he have? What kind of man was he if he couldn't provide, couldn't protect, couldn't even keep himself from falling into a hole?

The cougar screamed again, the sound reverberating through the cave, and August pressed his back against the cold stone.

"August?"

Felicity's voice pulled him back again, gentle but insistent. He realized they'd stopped walking, that he was gripping her hand too tightly.

He loosened his hold but didn't let go. "I'm sorry. I was—"

"I know." Her thumb stroked across the back of his hand, soothing. "You're here now. We're together."

He would thank God every day that she hadn't been harmed by the wildcat. He was eternally grateful for her by his side in this moment.

He didn't know what the future held. He couldn't scout anymore. Couldn't read tracks or spot danger or do any of the things that had made him valuable to the company. What was he supposed to do when they reached Oregon? How was he supposed to provide for Felicity and Ben?

"I don't know what's ahead," he admitted quietly. "I don't know how to be useful anymore. Don't know what I'm supposed to do."

"You're supposed to let me help you," Felicity said, her voice fierce now. "You're supposed to trust that we'll figure it out together. Not alone, August. Together."

The word settled into his chest, warm and solid.

Together.

In that cave, he'd been alone with his fear and his pain and his certainty that he had nothing left to offer. But he wasn't in that cave anymore. He was with Felicity, her hand in his, with Ben nearby playing with her friends, with a whole community of people who had searched for him and refused to give up.

Maybe the future would look different than he'd planned, but he wasn't worthless.

He was loved. And that was enough to start building a future on.

"Together," August repeated, testing the word. Believing it.

Felicity made a sound that might have been a laugh or a sob —maybe both. Then she stepped closer. August felt her forehead rest against his shoulder.

He wrapped his arms around her, holding her the way he

should have been holding her all along. His wife. The woman who had never stopped looking for him, even when he'd been lost in more ways than one.

"I love you," he said into her hair. "I should have been saying that every day."

"You can start now," she whispered back.

So he did. Into her hair, her shoulder, her cheek just before she went on tiptoe and met his lips in a kiss. Joy stretched through him. More when she broke the kiss to whisper, "I'll never stop loving you."

He stood in the joy and relief of it for a long moment.

"Come on," Felicity said with a soft laugh, pulling back slightly but keeping one hand in his. "Ben will be worried if we're gone too long."

August let her lead him forward, his steps steadier now. Not because the ground was any smoother, but because he wasn't walking alone anymore.

Whatever the future held, they would face it together.

* * *

Rob shifted on the crate, easing his healing leg into a better position. The evening sky was a riot of colors. Towering clouds banked on the far horizon, their underbellies stained crimson and gold by the setting sun. The color bled across the entire western sky, painting everything —wagons, canvas covers, even the dust—in shades of amber.

Only a handful of days left on the trail. The thought sent a thrill through him. After months of travel, of endless miles and exhaustion, they were almost there. Almost to the Willamette Valley.

The borrowed books from Evangeline lay open on either side of his sketch. One showed the inner workings of a water-wheel mechanism, the other a floor plan of a two-story sawmill. His pencil moved across fresh paper, the new plans taking shape.

"My father's first mill had the living quarters on the second floor." Evangeline's voice pulled his attention. She sat mending one of Sarah's dresses, her needle flashing in the firelight. "But the sawdust would drift up through the floorboards something terrible. Made Mother sneeze constantly."

Rob made a note in the margin. The books showed him mechanics. But Evangeline had lived it.

"Papa tried everything. Sealed boards, canvas barriers." Her needle kept moving, quick and practiced. "Nothing worked until he moved the living space to a separate addition. He connected them by a covered walkway."

Rob adjusted his sketch. The new plans were different than his originals—better, he thought. More real. The old plans had been drawn in his grandfather's study, all textbook knowledge and careful calculations. These were being born beside a wagon wheel in the wilderness.

"The kitchen." Evangeline studied his drawing. "You'll want it on the north side if you can manage it. Keeps it cooler in summer when you're running the wood stove."

He made another adjustment. His eye caught on the plucked grouse sitting in the pot beside him, ready for cooking, the tedious work already done. A small thing. But Alice would notice.

"What're you working on, Braddock?"

Rob looked up. Owen approached, baby Molly drowsing against his shoulder. Collin followed, one hand supporting Stella's elbow as she moved slowly, still healing.

"New sawmill plans."

"Let's see." Owen peered over his shoulder, then whistled low. "That's some house."

Heat crept up Rob's neck. "It needs to be functional. Alice will need proper workspace, and room for—"

"Oh, you'll definitely want a separate parlor." Collin settled Stella on a blanket near Evangeline, his movements careful. "A formal one. For entertaining."

Rob's pencil paused. "A parlor?"

"Sure." Collin dropped beside Stella, found her hand. "Ladies like that sort of thing. Somewhere fancy to receive guests."

Owen nodded, but Rob caught the glimmer in his eyes. "And you'll need a separate dining room. Can't have family meals in the kitchen—that's not proper."

"Alice grew up eating in—"

"Exactly." Owen shifted Molly. "Now's her chance to have something better. Something refined." He paused. "You should probably add a morning room too. I've heard fine ladies need a morning room."

Rob looked down at his sketch. Uncertainty crept in. He'd been drawing what he thought Alice would want—practical, warm, space for family. But what if Owen was right?

His pencil moved. He added another room. Then another.

"Don't forget the library," Collin said. "Every proper house needs a library."

"And a music room." Owen's voice was solemn. "Separate from the main living area, naturally."

Rob sketched faster. The house grew larger, more elaborate. This was what Alice deserved, wasn't it? After years of servitude, of work-roughened hands—

He glanced up.

Rachel stood near Owen, one hand pressed to her mouth. Her shoulders shook. Beside her, Stella had her lips pressed together, eyes dancing as she shook her head at Collin.

Rob's pencil stilled.

The brothers were grinning at each other.

"You're—" Heat flooded Rob's face. "You're teasing me."

"Little bit," Owen admitted.

"Alice doesn't want a morning room." Collin's grin widened. "She'd probably use it to store preserves."

Rob stared at them. He'd seen this before—watched the brothers rib each other over everything. Leo bore the brunt of it, the oldest an easy target.

But they'd never directed it at Rob.

Something warm bloomed in his chest.

Owen's grin softened. "We're just saying, Alice isn't your grandfather's crowd. She's not going to want something that needs a staff of servants."

"Though she'd probably like a big kitchen," Collin offered. "She does love to feed people."

"And good windows," Stella said quietly.

Rob looked back at his overlarge sketch. All these rooms. Alice would see exactly what they represented—years of scrubbing floors, dusting mantles, polishing silver in houses that had never been homes.

He reached for fresh paper.

"Starting over?" Evangeline asked.

"Starting better."

This time his pencil moved with confidence. A kitchen—generous but not cavernous. A main living area with space for family to gather. Bedrooms for children someday, but not wasteful. The covered walkway to the mill. Windows on the eastern side where Alice could catch morning light.

The house took shape. Smaller than before but somehow more right. More like a home.

He was focused on the drawing when her hand settled warm on his shoulder.

"What are you working on?"

Rob looked up. The easy affection in her touch—casual, comfortable, natural as breathing—sent satisfaction through him.

"New plans."

She leaned over his shoulder, her chin nearly brushing his ear. Her fingers tightened. "These aren't the same as before."

"No." He reached up, covered her hand with his. "The old plans were my grandfather's vision with my hand. These are *ours*."

"He tried to add a morning room," Collin said. "And a music room. And a library."

"And a formal parlor," Owen added.

Alice was quiet. Then, softly: "That's a lot of rooms. And I've scrubbed enough floors for a lifetime."

Rob twisted to look up at her.

Her eyes were bright. But she was smiling—that warm, genuine smile that transformed her whole face. "I don't need something big and fancy to be happy, Rob. I just need to be with you."

The tightness in his chest loosened. "You're sure?"

"Look at this." She pointed to the kitchen. "This is perfect. This is *us*. Room enough to live and work and raise a family, but not so much we'd rattle around in it like strangers."

"The kitchen's on the north side," Evangeline said. "Keeps it cooler."

"And there's the covered walkway." Rob showed her. "So you won't have to go outside in bad weather."

Alice traced the lines with her finger. Her expression softened. "You've been thinking about this. Really planning it."

"Every day."

She noticed the pot then. Her eyebrows rose. "Is that—did you pluck that bird?"

"Collin shot it this morning." Rob's ears heated. "I thought I could help with supper."

Owen snorted. "Thought we'd never see the day a Braddock plucked a grouse."

"Owen," Rachel chided. But she was smiling.

"I'm just saying, that's love right there." Owen grinned at Rob. "Man plucks a bird for a woman, he's serious."

"Owen's never plucked anything in his life," Collin said. "Rachel does all his birds."

"That's not—I've plucked plenty of—" Owen sputtered. Rachel laughed outright.

Alice looked at Rob a wondering expression. "You did this for me."

"It needed doing." He shrugged. "And you do everything else."

She glanced at her brothers, their wives, Evangeline still stitching. Then back at Rob. Warmth in her gaze made his breath catch.

"Thank you," she said quietly. "For the bird. And for the plans."

Collin drew Owen and Rachel into conversation as Evangeline took Sarah off to their wagon.

Alice moved around to kneel beside his crate. She studied the sketch, fingers tracing the careful lines.

"Show me everything. I want to see all of it."

So he did. The kitchen workspace. The eastern windows. The space he'd left undefined. "I wasn't sure what you'd want here. A sewing room? A place for—"

"A nursery." Color rose in Alice's cheeks. "Eventually."

"Eventually." His voice came out rough.

She was quiet. Then looked up at him. "We're going to build something beautiful. Together."

"Together."

She started to rise, but he caught her hand. "Alice, wait. Look here." He pointed to a detail added that morning. "I was thinking about your mother. About how you said she used to sing while she worked."

Her breath caught.

"What if there was space here for music? Room for Collin's fiddle, for singing." He traced the open floor plan. "A place where the house could be filled with the sounds of family. Where you could remember her."

* * *

Alice's eyes misted. If she'd needed any confirmation that being with Rob was the right thing, here it was. He was thinking about music, about her mother's memory.

When he caught sight of the moisture in her eyes, his expression changed to concern. "Alice? If you don't want a music room, we won't have one."

She pressed her fingertips to her lips. Took a breath. Said, "Wait for me? Just—wait here a moment."

She gathered her skirts and hurried toward Leo's wagon. Her hands were shaking as she climbed inside.

The interior was dim, the canvas cover blocking most of the fading light. Alice moved to where her few belongings were stowed in a crate near the back. She pushed aside her spare dress, her mother's shawl, the small bundle of letters from home that she'd carried all this way.

There.

The brown-wrapped package that she'd attempted to give back to Rob more than once. She'd kept it, hidden it away like a secret. Like hope she was too afraid to claim.

Alice pulled the package free from the crate, hands trembling as she untied the twine and the fabric unfurled. Even in the dim light, it gleamed. Beautiful. Expensive.

Her fingers found the buttons at the back of her work dress. They fumbled only a little as she undid them. She stepped out of the worn fabric—practical, durable, meant for labor—and left it pooled on the wagon bed.

The blue dress slid over her head easily.

Someone had set a half-full pail of water inside the wagon bed near the tailgate and in the fading light, Alice caught a glimpse of herself in the water's reflection.

The last time she'd worn a dress like this, she'd hidden in a linen closet. Terrified. Certain she didn't belong.

She'd felt exposed. Visible in a way that made her want to disappear.

Now—

Now she looked at herself and saw something different.

She still wasn't Miss Pence with her refined beauty and practiced manners. Alice's hands remained work-roughened. The freckles across her nose hadn't faded. That small scar under her chin was still there.

But she belonged in this dress.

Not because the fabric was fine or the cut was elegant. But because Rob had chosen her. Because he saw past the maid's work dress to the woman underneath. Because when he looked at her, he saw *Alice*—and that was enough.

More than enough.

She pressed her palm flat against her stomach, felt her heart hammering beneath her ribs. She was really going to do this.

When she'd climbed out of the wagon and returned to Rob, the sky had deepened to crimson and violet. The camp was settling into evening routines—fires crackling, low voices, the occasional laugh from children playing before bedtime.

He was still sitting on that crate where she'd left him, carefully closing up the books he'd spread at his side. He looked up at the sound of her approach.

His expression transformed, eyes going wide.

He pushed to his feet—awkward with the crutch, his healing leg making the movement slow. But his eyes never left her face.

"Alice." Her name came out rough. Wondering.

She stopped a few feet away, suddenly uncertain.

"I kept it," she blurted. "Maybe I should've sent it back with your grandfather—"

"You shouldn't have. It was a gift." He took a step toward her, then another. Closed the distance between them until he stood right in front of her. "You look beautiful."

Heat flooded her cheeks. "It's just a dress."

"No." His free hand came up to cup her face, his thumb brushing across her cheekbone. "It's you. It's always you."

Her breath caught.

This was the moment. She could feel it in her bones—the certainty, the rightness of what she was about to do.

Alice held his gaze and said, "I think we should get married."

Rob blinked. Surprise flickered across his face, followed quickly by something that looked like joy. Then—too quickly—his expression shuttered.

"Alice, I have no income." His voice was careful. "No savings to build us a house. Everything I had is gone."

"I don't care. This partnership with Leo and Evangeline is going to work." She spoke with a quiet determination. "We'll build the mill together. We'll make a life together." Her grip tightened on his hand. "And I don't want to wait any longer."

Rob stared at her. She watched as the practical worry gave way to something deeper. Something that looked like wonder.

"How can I refuse?" His voice came out barely above a whisper.

His hand slipped free from hers, but only so he could cup her face again with both hands. His crutch clattered to the ground, forgotten. He leaned in slowly, giving her time to pull away.

She didn't.

His lips met hers—gentle, reverent. A question and an answer all at once.

When he pulled back, his forehead rested against hers. "I love you, Alice Spencer."

"I love you too." The words felt like freedom.

Only a few minutes later, Owen had grudgingly fetched Hollis and gathered the family so that they stood in a rough circle near the fire. Leo and Evangeline with little Sarah between them. Collin supporting Stella, her hand resting over his heart. Owen with baby Molly drowsing on his shoulder, Rachel beside him. August and Felicity, with Ben clinging to her mother's skirt.

Hollis stood across from Alice and Rob, his worn Bible open in his hands.

Alice's eyes swept the gathered faces. Her family. The people who'd become family on this long journey west.

But where was—?

Coop was nowhere to be seen.

Her breath caught as the pang of hurt hit, sharp and sudden.

Rob was watching her closely. Of course he saw. He always saw too much. He leaned close, turning his shoulders so that the others wouldn't hear. "You brought August back into the fold when everyone but Felicity had given up on him."

Alice gazed at her soon-to-be-husband's dear face.

"You'll do the same with Coop." Rob's voice held certainty. "However long it takes."

Her anxiety eased. Not the sadness—that was still there, would probably be there for a while yet. But the fear underneath it loosened its grip.

Whatever came, Rob would be beside her. Not trying to fix it for her. Not dismissing her worry. Just... there. Steady. Present.

"Thank you," she whispered.

His hand found hers, their fingers lacing together.

Hollis cleared his throat. "Shall we begin?"

Alice nodded. Rob squeezed her hand.

Hollis's voice washed over her, deep and warm, as he led them through their vows. She welcomed the weight of Rob's hand in hers, his now callused palm rough against her work-worn fingers. The crackle of the fire behind them, sending up sparks that drifted into the darkening sky.

She heard Rob's responses—steady, sure, his voice never wavering even when Hollis asked him to pledge his life, his future, everything he had.

Her own voice was strong and clear. "I will."

The words felt like a vow and a claim all at once.

Around them, she was dimly aware of her family—Leo's quiet pride, Evangeline's soft smile, the way Collin had his arm around Stella as if holding her up. August standing tall beside Felicity, Ben tucked against her side.

This was her family. Not just by blood, but by choice. By the long miles they'd traveled together, the hardships endured, the grace extended even when it wasn't deserved.

And Rob—Rob who'd left everything behind for her. Who'd faced his grandfather's rejection and counted it worth the cost. Who folded paper hearts and made grand plans.

Rob, who saw her.

Then Hollis's voice cut through her wonder: "I now pronounce you man and wife."

A pause. The whole world seemed to hold its breath.

"You may kiss your bride."

Rob's hand came up to cup her face, the gesture achingly familiar now. His thumb traced her cheekbone before he leaned in and kissed her. His wife.

This kiss was a homecoming. She belonged to Rob. And he belonged to her. His arm came around her waist, drawing her close. Alice's hands came up to grip his shoulders, steadying herself against the tide of emotion.

Around them, her family cheered. Owen let out a whoop that made Molly startle and fuss. Sarah clapped her hands. Ben laughed.

But Alice barely heard it.

Because this—this moment, this man, this impossible, outrageous love—this was real.

Rob pulled back just far enough to rest his forehead against hers. His eyes were bright with unshed tears.

"My wife," he said, testing out the words.

"My husband." Alice smiled, felt tears slip free to track down her own cheeks.

The Willamette Valley was only days away now. The house they'd sketched on paper would take months—maybe years— to build. There would be hard work ahead. Struggles she couldn't yet imagine. Wounds still to heal, like the one Coop carried.

But they'd face it together.

Alice Spencer—Alice *Braddock* now—looked at her

husband in the firelight and knew with absolute certainty that this was the life God had been writing for her all along. Not the one she'd imagined back in New Jersey, scrubbing floors in the Braddock household. Not the future she'd thought she wanted.

Something better.

Home wasn't a place.

It was this man. This family. This moment suspended between sunset and starlight, between the journey behind them and the life stretching ahead.

It was enough.

More than enough.

It was everything.

Epilogue

"I NEED TO TALK TO YOU."

Belle jumped, whirling to face the man who'd approached.

Hollis. The wagon master. He loomed over her where she stood beside Doc and Maddie's wagon.

When he noticed her recoil, he inched back slightly. But he was so tall and broad—if he really meant her harm, she didn't stand a chance.

The sun had dropped below the western mountains, leaving the camp bathed in that gray twilight that made every shadow look like a threat. Fires flickered to life around the circled wagons, but offered little comfort. Not when Jason and Maddie were away from the wagon, doctoring folks.

Since she'd come out of the caves with Coop, Belle had kept close to this wagon. She'd stayed inside as much as she could, using the excuse of wrangling baby Jenny during the day because of the rough terrain. She'd heard a whisper between

Maddie and Jason that Sarge had been spotted in the fog. The one who'd taken shots at Coop.

Most times when Belle'd been outside the wagon, Coop had been nearby. Always watching.

She didn't know how to feel about him now. Back in the cave, he'd given her his gun. What if she'd tried to use it on him? She could've.

And he'd never asked for it back. She kept it near all the time.

That same morning after they'd been found, Alex and Paul had discovered a brown paper-wrapped package beneath the wagon wheel in camp. They'd chattered how it had her name scrawled on the paper. Not that she could read her own name.

She'd opened it to find a woolen shawl. Perfectly service-able, warm. She suspected it was from Coop, but why wouldn't he have just given it to her? Maybe she shouldn't wear it. A gift meant an exchange. But the weather had grown so cold...

Hollis cleared his throat.

Belle refocused on him, realizing she'd been staring at him. Lost in her swirling thoughts. She wrapped her arms around herself inside the shawl, hugging herself tight.

"Having you as a part of the company has caused a lot of trouble for us."

At his stern words, Belle started to shake. Horses stamped from somewhere nearby. A normal sound, but she still startled.

She didn't answer Hollis. Just watched his face—the lines around his mouth, the way his eyes wouldn't quite meet hers. He looked like he would rather be anywhere other than here.

"There's men who have gotten into a brawl because of

you." His voice was measured. Careful. "The man you say is after you—Sarge? He shot at one of my men."

Footsteps approached from behind the wagon. Out of habit, Belle's hand went to her pocket. To the knife. But it was just Jason and Maddie, joining their small circle.

"What exactly are you saying?" Jason asked, tone flat.

Maddie came to stand next to Belle, who had to force herself not to shrink back. Men who spoke the way Jason had often devolved into fistfights. In her experience.

Hollis didn't flinch. Spoke evenly. "As much as it pains me to say it, she can't stay on. She's a danger to the company. Caused quite a bit of trouble. There's a lot of complaints about having a—having her travel with us."

Having a woman like her around. That's what he'd meant to say before he'd stopped himself. The hollow feeling inside Belle opened wider.

"We're only a few weeks from the end of the trail," Maddie argued. "The company can't just abandon her."

"She was never a part of the company to begin with."

Maddie's chin came up stubbornly at Hollis's words, but Belle spoke before she could argue.

"He's right." The whispered words scraped her throat raw. "I should never have stowed away in your wagon."

Hollis shifted his feet. "It would be different if she belonged to somebody."

Those words cut somehow. Through hurts Belle thought long scarred over.

"If she was someone's daughter." He paused long enough for her to hear the fire crackle behind him. "Or if she was someone's wife."

"If she was married, you'd keep her on with the company?" Coop's voice came from the shadows between wagons. Only a moment later, the man himself emerged.

Belle's breath caught as her fingers twisted in the fabric of her shawl. It was obvious he'd been listening. There was something angry about the set of his jaw as he stepped into the circle of firelight, his broad shoulder brushing hers briefly.

Part of her wanted to step away. To run. But she couldn't move.

Coop's sideways glance flicked to her—just for a second— then settled on Hollis.

"What if I marry her?"

Maddie gasped. Small and sharp.

Coop still stared at Hollis. That stubborn set to his jaw that she'd seen before—when he'd faced down those two men, just before punches had started flying.

From the corner of her eye, Belle saw Jason grab Maddie's hand. To silence her?

Hollis's face had gone grim, the firelight casting hard shadows across his features. A log shifted in the fire, sending up sparks that drifted into the darkening sky.

"I think that's the only solution." Hollis's voice carried a tone that brooked no argument as he turned his face to look directly at Belle. "Either you get married or leave the wagon train."

* * *

Thank you for reading HEART'S PERILOUS JOURNEY. I

hope you loved Rob and Alice's romance. You'll see them again in LONG TRAIL HOME...

All roads lead home in the dramatic conclusion to one family's journey of love, sacrifice, and survival.

Since the moment he saw her, Coop Spencer has been single-minded in his quest to protect Belle. She's running from something—someone—and he's never met anyone so scared. When the wagon master forces an ultimatum: a marriage or Belle is expelled from the wagon train, Coop makes the only choice he can. He'll do everything in his power to prove he's the kind of man she can trust. But overcoming the mistakes of his past may prove too much...

Belle knows that the danger she escaped is still out there,

still hunting her. Experience has taught her that she can't rely on anyone, not even the man who promised their marriage was in name only.

As they traverse the Oregon Trail together, Belle is taken in by Coop's big family, and the more time she spends with her temporary husband and his siblings, the more she starts to long for something she'd forgotten ages ago: home.

When danger closes in, one of them must sacrifice everything for love...

- Forced marriage of convenience
- Redemption
- Family saga
- Heroine with a dark past/sworn off men

ONE CLICK LONG TRAIL HOME NOW >

Acknowledgments

As always, I'm grateful to my proofreaders Lillian, MaryEllen, Benecia, and Shelley for helping me clean up all the little errors (there were many!)—and do my early/advanced readers who caught even more that snuck through. A million thanks!

Want to connect online? Here's where you can find me:

GET NEW RELEASE ALERTS

Follow me on Amazon
Follow me on Bookbub
Follow me on Goodreads

CONNECT ON THE WEB

www.lacywilliams.net
lacy@lacywilliams.net

SOCIAL MEDIA

Snowbound at Christmas (anthology)

WIND RIVER LEGACY SERIES (HISTORICAL ROMANCE)

The Homesteader's Sweetheart

Roping the Wrangler

Return of the Cowboy Doctor

The Wrangler's Inconvenient Wife

A Cowboy for Christmas

Her Convenient Cowboy

Her Cowboy Deputy

Catching the Cowgirl

The Cowboy's Honor

Winning the Schoolmarm

The Wrangler's Ready-Made Family

Christmas Homecoming

Heart of Gold

Courted by a Cowboy

WIND RIVER HEARTS SERIES (HISTORICAL ROMANCE)

Marrying Miss Marshal

Counterfeit Cowboy

Cowboy Pride

SUTTER'S HOLLOW SERIES
(CONTEMPORARY ROMANCE)

His Small-Town Girl

Secondhand Cowboy

The Cowgirl Next Door

CONTEMPORARY COWBOY BOX SETS
(CONTEMPORARY ROMANCE)

Three Cowboy Christmas Wishes

Three Sweethearts for Three Rodeo Brothers

Three Inconvenient Wedding Dates

Three Matches for Three Cowboy Brothers

Three Grooms for Three Cowgirls

Three Second Chance Cowboys

Three Small Town Sweethearts

Five Cowboy Royals

Five Brides for Five Hometown Ranchers

Four Cowboy Royals

Copyright © 2025 by Lacy Williams

All rights reserved.

No part of this book may be reproduced in any form or by any electronic or mechanical means, including information storage and retrieval systems, without written permission from the author, except for the use of brief quotations in a book review.